D1617496

FRAME AND THE MCGUIRE

FRAME AND THE MCGUIRE

JOANNA M. WESTON

VANCOUVER LONDON

Text © 2015 by Joanna M. Weston
Cover illustration © 2015 by Kim La Fave
Cover design by Elisa Gutiérrez
Book design by Jacqueline Wang

Published in the UK in 2015
Published in the USA in 2016

Mixed Sources
Cert no. SW-COC-001271
© 1996 FSC
FSC

Inside pages printed on FSC certified paper using vegetable-based inks.

Printed in Canada by Sunrise Printing

2 4 6 8 10 9 7 5 3 1

Cataloguing-in-Publication Data for this book is available from The British Library.

Library and Archives Canada Cataloguing in Publication

Weston, Joanna M., 1938-, author
Frame and the McGuire / Joanna M. Weston.

ISBN 978-1-896580-59-3 (paperback)

I. Title.

PS8595.E75F73 2015   jC813'.54   C2015-903076-5

For my Peacewoode family —

with thanks always to Robert for listening

Tradewind Books thanks the Governments of Canada and British Columbia for the financial support they have extended through the Canada Book Fund, Livres Canada Books, the Canada Council for the Arts, the British Columbia Arts Council Council, Creative BC and the British Columbia Book Publishing Tax Credit program.

Canada Council
for the Arts

Conseil des Arts
du Canada

BRITISH COLUMBIA
ARTS COUNCIL
Supported by the Province of British Columbia

LIVRES CANADA BOOKS

CHAPTER 1

IT COULD BE AN OLD SHIRT. BUT IT'S a jacket. And there's a sleeve with an arm inside, and a hand. There's a tattoo on the back of the hand. I know that tattoo.

"Ranger! Ranger!" I yell. I can't take my eyes off it.

The run of the river is so loud I don't hear Ranger until he's right beside me. I point, my hand shaking. My voice comes out in a croak. "Look," I say.

Dead leaves, a plastic bag and twigs hurtle past on the flood. A branch bends into the water, a bundle of river litter caught against it. Plaid cloth billows up, and something white.

Ranger gasps. "It's a body!"

"It's Uncle Tam's jacket." I'm shaking. "What do we do?" I wipe my nose on my sleeve.

"Tell the Piercys. They'll know what to do." Ranger sniffs. "You stay here."

"Why do I have to stay?"

"To make sure he doesn't drift away. Just stay

here." Ranger takes off, his feet slopping in the sodden ground.

I stumble backward against a tree. Thin February sunlight gleams on the wave crests. The river is in full flood, high and rushing between its banks. A branch whirls past me.

I can't take my eyes away from Uncle Tam. He's not our real uncle; he's a family friend. He lives beyond the train station, across the river from the Dakens.

But he doesn't live there anymore. He's in the river, drowned. He won't give his talk about fire safety at our school next year. He won't volunteer with the Cowichan Station fire department again, or drink hot chocolate with us, or build a radio, or tell funny jokes. I have to think of him as in the past.

I'm going to be sick. I bite my knuckles, then suck the end of my ponytail.

The branch sways, locked against the bend. Uncle Tam's jacket balloons with the current, and sinks again. His red-brown hair is twisted up in the twigs.

I close my eyes. I wish I'd gone home from school with Amanda, my best friend. I wish Ranger and I hadn't looked over the bridge, seen a tennis ball, and decided to fish it out of the river. I wish . . . It seems like hours and hours go by before Ranger comes back with Mr. Piercy.

He takes one horrified look and says, "Okay, kids, you go up to the house. Tell Mrs. Piercy to call the police."

We race up to the Piercy house, scrambling under the fence along their driveway. Mrs. Piercy is standing on the front step, with Stephie beside her. Bingo barks inside the house.

"Mr. Piercy says to call the police," Ranger says.

"Heavens above!" says Mrs. Piercy.

"It's Uncle Tam," says Ranger.

"Is he really dead?" Stephie asks as her mother goes back into the house.

I stand behind Ranger's shoulder for protection from Stephie: she teases me at school. Ranger has often saved me from her bullying. I'm nervous, scared and shy. I curl my hands inside my pockets and rub one wet muddy runner up and down my leg.

Mrs. Piercy comes out. "The police will be here soon. And I've called your Ma. She's coming right over to get you."

"Thanks," says Ranger. "We'll meet her by the bridge. Our back-packs are there."

"Are you okay, then?"

I curl my toes up and look down.

"Yes," Ranger says. He turns to Stephie. "See you tomorrow, Stephie."

We get to the bridge just as Ma arrives. She parks, gets out and bundles Ranger and me into her arms, holding us tight.

"That was bad, bad, bad," she says.

I start to cry.

Slowly, Ma opens her arms, takes a good look at us and gives us tissues.

"What a thing to happen," she says. "Awful."

I blow my nose and sniff. Ranger rubs his eyes.

"Get in and let's go home," Ma says.

We dump our packs in the back of the pickup and climb onto the front seat with Squib wedged between us. She's our four-year-old sister, adopted from Russia when she was a baby.

I lean my head against Ma and wish it was a normal school day. I wish Uncle Tam's body didn't rise and fall with the current. I stare out the car window and blow my nose. Ranger ties knots in a piece of string and doesn't speak. Squib sucks one paw of her beloved Teddy Bear.

Ma glances at me. "You found him, Frame?"

"Yes."

"There was a tennis ball," Ranger says. He stuffs the string in one pocket and pulls the tennis ball out of another.

"We saw it from the bridge," I say.

"We didn't get wet." Ranger rolls the tennis ball in his hands.

"There was some fishing line . . ."

"We always find good stuff when the river is high," Ranger says.

"Right down where the river bends there was a fallen tree and a pile up of branches, and that's where . . ." My voice trails away; tears trickle into my mouth.

Ma drives up Riverside, past Amanda's home, round the steep corner at Curzon's place at speed. "You feel like you'd been kicked in the stomach?"

"Yes."

"Me too." She pulls into our driveway and we get out, go into the house and settle on stools at the kitchen counter. I stare out the window, up to the barns. No one says a word while Ma makes hot chocolate. It thaws the cold feeling in my stomach. Squib sits and hugs Bear while eating a cookie. Tucker, our sort-of-Labrador, comes out from his basket in the sitting room and puts his nose against my hand. I scratch his head.

"It was so . . . so . . . horrid, Ma. I mean, it's *Uncle Tam*," I say.

She runs her hands through her red hair and rubs her eyes. "I know. I can't believe it."

13

I can't believe I found him. But I can't get what I saw out of my head.

"Uncle Tam's hair floated out," says Ranger.

I shiver. "His jacket filled with air . . ."

"He gave us Primrose," says Ranger. Primrose is our best milk cow.

"He gave me that frilly doll last Christmas," I say and blow my nose again. I hate dolls but Uncle Tam gave it to me, so I kept it.

"He was just one good guy," Ma says, picking up the phone. "I'd better call your sister and tell her what happened. She should come home for the funeral."

My sister, Bird, is at university in Victoria. I miss her a lot.

Then our car drives up, and Pa and Michael come in. Ma tells them about Uncle Tam. Pa holds Ma tight. Michael sits on a stool at the counter with his head in his hands.

Someone knocks at the front door. Michael gets up slowly and opens it to find two police officers filling the doorway. They give their names, which I don't catch, and say they're from the Duncan police station.

Michael puts a hand on Tucker, bringing him close. Tucker is more Michael's dog than mine even though it was me that found Tucker by the roadside, a shivering puppy, and brought him home three years ago.

The short thin officer says, "I understand your family knew Thomas Sinclair well?"

"We went to school together in Edinburgh," Ma says. "Then I was his taxi-driver, pure coincidence, when he came looking for land in the valley."

"I'm really sorry for your loss," says Short Thin. "And I apologize for having to ask questions. I would like to talk to the kids who found Mr. Sinclair in the river."

"That's us," Ranger says. I stand up next to him and stare at the big tall officer's muddy shoes. Ranger tells them what happened.

"Okay, thanks, kids," Short Thin says. He turns to Ma and asks, "Mrs. Williams, is there anything about Mr. Sinclair that the police should know?"

"Not that I can think of," says Ma. "Why? Is something suspicious about his death?"

"We're looking into it," says Big Tall.

Pa glances at Ma. "He had friends in Alberta."

"His ranch was there," Ma says.

Big Tall scribbles in his notebook, then looks up and says, "I'm truly sorry, but there will have to be an inquest. It'll probably be early next week, just as soon as we can get all the information we need. If you could jot down the names of anyone he knew, that would be helpful."

"There was a break-in last night at the Dakens' place," Ma says as they turn to go.

"Yes, we're investigating that," Short Thin says.

"Their collection of Victorian coins was taken," Pa says. "It was very valuable."

Ranger pokes me. "Why would anyone want to take a bunch of old coins?" he asks.

"Only the gold coins were taken," says Ma.

Big Tall looks down at Ranger and says, "And they could be sold for a lot of money, no questions asked."

"If we need any more information, we'll give you a call," Short Thin says.

Pa nods. The officers leave and I turn to Ma.

"Were the horses hurt?" I ask. I help at the Dakens' riding stable, grooming the horses and cleaning the stables. I dream of having my own, my very own horse.

Ma ruffles my hair and says, "No, they're fine."

Pa sits down at the counter. He runs his hands through his hair. "Seth Curzon is out of work right now; he'd be the best person to look after Tam's place."

"You're right," Ma says. "He took care of it before when Tam was away,"

Pa picks up the phone, calls Seth and asks, "Can you look after Uncle Tam's farm for a while?"

I follow the conversation by the pauses: Seth asks what happened, why he's needed. Pa explains. Then

Pa says, "It's true. Would you stay in Tam's house? How soon can you be there?"

Another pause and Pa says, "Okay, I'll meet you at Tam's as soon as I can."

I can't get over the idea of Uncle Tam being dead. I feel as if I've been hit over the head with a baseball bat.

Michael and Ranger go upstairs to the room they share. I take Squib downstairs and huddle with her.

I can still see Uncle Tam's body rise and fall.

That night I wake up yelling. Ma comes in and hugs me.

"It's the way his body moved in the river." I sob.

She doesn't say anything, just holds me until I stop shaking and fall back to sleep.

CHAPTER 2

MORNING COMES AND IT'S TUESDAY, another school day, and no, I can't stay home, though I try. Pa says, "You have to deal with it at school, and the sooner, the better. And stay together on the road. I mean it—stay together."

So Ranger and I leave as usual, the sky grey and curdled. And there's Amanda, waiting at the end of her driveway, hopping from one foot to the other, brown hair floating out in a fizz of curls. Her lime-green pants and fluorescent blue jacket make the sky look even darker.

Ranger runs off ahead of us.

I yell, "Pa says we're to stay together." But he's round the corner already. We follow him. "We'd better keep Ranger in sight," I say.

"So you found Uncle Tam," Amanda says. "We'll all miss him. What's it like seeing a dead person? Must have been like being kicked by a horse. Did you throw up? Did you hear about the break-in at the Dakens'?"

"Yes." I answer the last question as we jog down the hill. "And no, I didn't throw up."

"You've got owl-eyes this morning." She studies my face. "Did you have nightmares all night?"

"Yes."

She's silent for almost ten seconds, then says, "I still dream about Mum."

Amanda's mum died of cancer two years ago. Her uncle and aunt moved in with them to help her dad work the farm.

I stare at her; she's looking straight ahead. Then she hops, skips a couple of steps and says, "You'll get interrogated by the police. You know that don't you? You might have to go to the police station!" Amanda looks into my eyes, her light-brown eyes close to mine. "My dad won't even let me go to school on my own; I have to wait for you every single day. He's scared I'll get pole-axed or kidnapped or eaten by bears."

I laugh. Yesterday I didn't think I'd ever laugh again. Amanda makes me feel better.

"Do you remember riding on the fire truck when they brought it to school for a fire drill?" Amanda continues. "Wasn't that fun? Uncle Tam let me ride in the driver's seat. He had a tattoo of a spider on the back of his hand that moved its legs when he clenched his fingers."

I remember the back of his hand in the river, how the water lifted his arm, the tattoo in the sunlight. I shudder.

We turn the corner at the bottom of the road and slow to a walk. Ranger joins up with two other kids ahead of us.

"My dad says he was 'filthy rich,'" Amanda says. "And that he knew lots about cows because of that cattle ranch he used to have, eons ago."

Amanda hasn't stopped talking. "And we bought a cow from him last year at the auction—that's Blossom, and she's due to calve next month, and we're going to have it for beef 'no matter what,' my dad says."

I don't look at the river when we cross the bridge. Amanda stops to hang over the rail. She wants me to point out where I found Uncle Tam's body.

I shake my head. "You can't see it from here."

"There's police tape along the bank," Amanda says. She catches up with me by the Piercy's driveway.

The school buzzes with the news. Kids from other grades ask me what happened and I have to answer. They've all met Uncle Tam.

I feel quivery inside and miserable. I try hiding in the washroom but have to go to class. At recess I find a tree in the corner of the playing field and hide behind that. Ranger gets bombarded with questions.

Stephie talks about everything she saw. She tells about the police coming, the police tape along the river, police searching for clues, asking questions, and about the body being taken away in an ambulance. She loves every minute of it.

I almost miss the math test on Wednesday because Stephie puts gum in my ponytail and I have to pull it out. I wish I'd missed the test. For me, numbers don't stay in one place; they add themselves up in funny ways and the answer is never the same twice.

At lunchtime, the school is still buzzing: it was announced on the radio that Uncle Tam didn't drown. He was stabbed—stabbed in the chest.

The rest of the week I'm in a fog, muddled and confused. Why would anyone murder Uncle Tam? Pa repeats that Ranger and I have to walk everywhere together for our own safety.

Uncle Tam knew everyone in Cowichan Station, volunteered for the fire department when he came to live here after he sold his ranch. Him being killed doesn't make any sense.

I go horse-riding with the Dakens on Saturday. They tell me more about the break-in—a broken window and their gold coins taken. And, to make everything worse, Uncle Tam's dog Sandy is missing. He went everywhere with Uncle Tam.

The days blur between overcast skies and a storm that takes a tree down. Ma and Pa spend a lot of time at Uncle Tam's farm, sorting things out, with Seth Curzon helping. They find a calf, the escape artist, in the woods at the back of the property. He's back in the barn, corralled for now.

The inquest happens the following week, on Thursday. Ranger and I don't have to go as Mr. and Mrs. Piercy both identified Uncle Tam at the river. So we go to school as usual. Pa tells us over dinner that they haven't found out who killed Uncle Tam. Ma picks at her fried chicken and says nothing.

"What did they find out?" Michael asks.

"The police say he drowned after he was stabbed," says Pa.

"What else did they say?" asks Ranger.

"They think it might be something to do with the break-in at the Dakens'. He could have seen who did it," says Pa.

"Finch says there were broken willow branches along the river at Tam's place . . . at the bottom of the path to the river," Ma says. "Anyway, we have the funeral to arrange. It'll be Tuesday next week."

I wish the sadness would go away, that Uncle Tam hadn't died, that everything could be normal again. I wish he'd drop in to help Pa with the fencing, or call to grumble about the calf that was always running off.

Pa phones the local paper about the funeral, and then spends the evening on the phone calling people.

CHAPTER 3

NEXT DAY, WE COME DOWN THE ROAD from the school to the bridge. I stop and lean on the rail, watch the run of water and think of Uncle Tam.

Ranger says, "We could go along the bank and check for clues."

"The police have already done that, so it'd be a waste of time."

"I suppose we can't go under the police tape anyway," Ranger grumbles.

We've got as much hope of discovering who killed Uncle Tam as I have of getting a hundred percent on a math test.

There's nothing we can do tonight anyway: we've got homework and chores to do. We go home, and everyone is quiet. I study and keep remembering Uncle Tam.

Then it's Saturday morning with cotton wool clouds floating across a blue sky. A breeze makes the tops of the maple trees dance. Sunlight gleams on Michael's red hair, the train tracks and the Scout knife hanging from Ranger's belt. We're at the train station with Tucker. There used to be a post office and hotel near the station. Now it's just part of a rural area: Cowichan Station, Vancouver Island, British Columbia, Canada, Earth, The Universe. I put my whole address, and the year, 1985, in all my Grade 5 books, the way all the girls in my class do.

Hands stuck in my pockets, I scuff and kick at the gravel. I'd like to get closer to the horses on the other side of the tracks, but the train from Victoria is due with Bird on board. She's the best big sister in the world. She used to share clothes and give me advice about school before she started at the University of Victoria. I miss her a lot. For Christmas she gave me the horse barrettes I'm wearing.

Tucker sniffs along the tracks.

Ranger has his ear to the rails, listening for the hum that tells when the train gets close. I stare down the track over Ranger's shoulder.

Ranger jumps up. "The train's coming."

The train-whistle echoes down the valley: a long lonely sound.

When the train pulls in, Bird is standing, almost

hidden, behind the conductor. She's tiny, half a head taller than me, and I'm only four feet tall. The conductor jumps down and places the step for her to come down. She's holding a pineapple. She brings the weirdest stuff for us.

Ranger hugs her and takes the pineapple from her, shouting, "It's prickly! It smells great!"

The train whistles and clatter-clunks its way up the track. Bird puts an arm round me briefly and rubs my shoulder, the way she always did. I swing her hand as we walk to the car, happy to have her back.

Michael puts Bird's bag in the trunk of the car and we pile in. Bird sits up front, Ranger and me in the back, and we do up seat belts. Everyone talks at once. Tucker squeezes in at Michael's feet.

Bird tries to answer questions, while looking out the window and fending off Tucker, who scrambles up and sticks his head out the window to bark at every passing smell.

I want to get close to Bird and tell her everything that's happened, so I lean forward and shout over Michael's shoulder, "We could show Bird, or at least point out, where . . . er . . . where we found Uncle Tam."

I feel like a ghoul.

Bird twists sideways to look at me. Her dark hair fluffs out, smelling faintly lemony.

"Tell me all about it," says Bird.

"It was awful," I say. And I don't want to go on.

We turn under the stone railway bridge and start down the hill.

"He was in the river," Ranger says. "We found a tennis ball."

Michael makes the turn onto Riverside Road so fast that I fall against Ranger. Michael got his licence last November and he likes to take curves like a racing driver, which is fun as Riverside winds a lot and is steep in places.

I straighten up and say, "Two police officers came to the house and we had to tell them what we saw."

"I think they wanted to know whether we'd messed up the crime scene," says Ranger.

"They interviewed everyone who lives on Riverside Road or along the river," Michael says.

"There's police tape along the river," I say.

Ranger says, "Stephie said there were police cars and an ambulance and a tracker dog."

I pitch against Ranger on a curve. Michael pulls into our driveway and we tumble out of the car.

Ma meets us in the kitchen. She and Bird hug hard. "Coffee's on and there's hot water for tea, Bird," says Ma.

"Where's Pa?" Bird asks.

"Had to get more hen-scratch and took Squib with him," says Ma.

Bird sits on a stool at the counter with everyone crowding round to catch up with her. She's not been home since Christmas. She's let her hair grow down below her ears; she used to have it cut like Julius Caesar. She's wearing a different colour lipstick—it's more purply—and a shirt I haven't seen before.

Having her come home is wonderful. But she's seen and done things I don't know about. She looks around, as if she expects everything to be different. She's not the same . . . and she'll leave again.

Ma pours coffee and makes a pot of tea for Bird, pushing it across the counter with one hand and taking the pineapple from Ranger with the other. "We'll keep that for dessert, Ranger," she says.

Bird wants to know more about Uncle Tam.

"He drowned, but it looks like he was in a fight before he fell in the river," says Ma. I picture blood seeping through his hair, dripping to the ground with a slow plop, and shiver.

"Have the police arrested anyone?" Bird asks.

"All of Tam's friends have been questioned, including us." She pauses to drink her coffee and then asks, "Couldn't your boyfriend come with you?"

"Leo? He wanted to, but he has an essay to write."

"Does he have a car?"

"Yes, sort of, he shares it with another guy," says Bird. "He works part-time . . . He's always busy so we don't see each other everyday."

"How long have you been going out with him?" Ma asks.

"Since before Thanksgiving."

I swirl my juice around in the glass, take a long drink, then plunk the glass down on the counter: turkey-toed Leo.

I paint a horse's head on the back of my math notebook with the black nail polish Amanda gave me last week. The horse has an angry face. I don't want to hear about Bird's boyfriend, or talk about him: I want Bird to be with me, to talk about Stephie and Uncle Tam.

"I think Mr. McGuire has got himself a dog," Michael says, taking a cookie.

"He wouldn't know how to look after a dog!" I say. The McGuire is one neighbour I don't like: he's big and shouts a lot.

"You don't know that," says Bird.

"Remember when he threw a garbage can lid at Tucker?" I say.

"Tucker was running around his yard, chasing his turkeys," Bird says.

"Still, no one should throw things at dogs. It's cruel," I reply.

"Well, Tucker doesn't go in his yard anymore," says Michael.

"When did he get the dog anyway?" I ask. I remember hearing a dog bark but didn't know where the sound came from.

"I heard a dog bark, when I went for the mail," Michael says. " I haven't seen it, though."

"I'll keep an eye out for it," I say, determined to check on the dog. Even The McGuire's turkeys worry me: they always look miserable, wandering around their run. "Bird, help me look for The McGuire's dog."

"It's The McGuire's dog, Frame, so leave it alone." There's a warning note in Ma's voice.

"That's right," says Bird. "It's *his* dog."

Bird always used to take my side; now she sounds just like Ma. I paint the horse's body, but there's not enough varnish left and the legs end up like knobby twigs. My dream horse, Midnight, would have strong legs.

Maybe Ranger will come with me to see The McGuire's dog. That will show Bird.

"Ranger, let's go see The McGuire's new dog."

"Sure, let's go."

"Stay off Mr. McGuire's property, both of you,"

says Ma. "He's a strange man."

"Okay, Ma," Ranger says.

"Michael," Ma says, "Pa said he'll need your help to fix the fence along the top field. Go up and see what you'll need to do it."

"Dagnabit!" says Michael. "Meet the unpaid farmhand: me."

"And who likes fresh cream in his coffee?"

"No peace for anyone around here," says Michael.

Ma laughs.

There's always something to be fixed. We live on a hobby-farm, with cows, chickens, and sometimes pigs. We raise a few turkeys for Thanksgiving and Christmas as well.

Michael, Ranger, and I push and shove to get our jackets and boots out of the cupboard by the front door and go outside. I can hear a dog barking somewhere near. Michael heads past the garden to the barnyard and the field beyond the barns.

"Let's sneak along the bank and come up at the back of his property," says Ranger. "That way, if he's home, he won't see us."

We go down the road, over the creek. The water rushes out of the culvert in a long tumbling tongue that breaks on a fallen tree trunk.

I follow Ranger, slithering down the bank on the other side of the road, almost falling into the creek. The sound of a dog barking gets louder as we worm our way through the underbrush. It's good that we're skinny and small like Pa; we can slide through gaps behind The McGuire's outbuildings at the back of his place.

There's a shacky-looking barn close to the woods and we stop in the bushes behind it. One of the vertical boards rattles and clatters in the wind. Blown shakes lie around among thistles, broken crates, and a rusted oil tank.

"There'll be nails in that lot," I murmur to Ranger.

The loose board bangs against the barn.

"Let's look inside," I say.

Ranger jumps up. I grab his jacket. "We don't want The McGuire to hear us."

We creep to the barn together, swing the loose board to one side and peer through the gap. Inside there's a mess of jumbled boxes, crates, broken incubators and rusted machinery. Rain drips from the roof; the place smells of old manure.

The door at the other end of the barn is missing and I can see all the way through to the outside. The dog, muddy, shrunken, scruffy, is tied to a post with no shelter at all, barking at us.

I study the dog. He looks familiar. "He looks sort of like Sandy."

"It couldn't be," Ranger mutters.

"I think it is," I whisper. "He's thin . . . he's the right size. And his colour is the same in a filthy dirty sort of way."

"It can't be him," says Ranger. "The McGuire wouldn't have Uncle Tam's dog."

"I'm sure it is: it's *Sandy*."

"He does look like him."

"It *is* Sandy. And he should have a kennel."

"We could cut him loose."

I creep along the side of the barn and look round the corner.

And there's The McGuire, his back to me, moving boxes from an old oil tank onto an even older-looking freezer behind it. His chequered jacket hangs crookedly, and his shoulder-length hair lifts in the wind. I jump back and bump into Ranger who bangs against the barn. The loose board swings and bangs loudly.

"He's there," I whisper, grabbing Ranger's jacket and dragging him out toward the bank. "Let's go."

CHAPTER 4

FOOTSTEPS CRASH ALONG THE SIDE of the barn. "What the hell are you doing here? Stop, the pair of you!"

I skid into a tree and Ranger cannons into me. For a moment I'm stuck, then Ranger shifts and I wriggle out from under him and we escape to the road. I look behind me.

At the top of the bank, The McGuire is standing with one hand raised in a fist as if he might be holding a stone to throw. "What are you kids doing here?"

"I thought I saw a mink," Ranger says.

I would never have thought of that.

"Stay away from my dog, he bites. He's a guard dog. And you've no damned business on my place anyway."

His raised hand drops slowly. The McGuire narrows his eyes. I hold my breath. "Get off my property and make sure you don't come here unless you're invited," he shouts.

Ranger slips and slides through the bushes on the river bank.

"He's mean," I say. "I wonder how he got hold of Sandy."

Ranger runs his fingers through his hair to get rid of the twigs and leaves. "How should I know? I guess he found him someplace."

"I suppose so," I say.

I look back at The McGuire's place. "I wonder why The McGuire keeps him tied up round the back of the house."

"He's weird," says Ranger. "And why do you think he was piling boxes on top of that old freezer?"

"Maybe he's hiding something?"

Ranger's eyes sparkle and he says, "We should go back, poke around and find out . . . because us being there sure made him mad."

I turn and run up the road, then down our driveway with Ranger on my heels. I wish I liked The McGuire.

Pa drives the truck in right behind us and jumps out. "Guess who was walking up here to visit?"

Amanda jumps out of the truck. Squib slides out behind her, clutching Bear.

"Don't tell Amanda about Sandy," I say quickly.

"That would be like telling the whole world," Ranger says.

"That means we can't tell Pa and Ma."

"We shouldn't have been snooping anyway." Ranger goes to help Pa take the chick scratch to the barn, and Amanda, wearing orange pants and a purple sweatshirt, dances over to me. She's talking nineteen to the million as always.

Amanda and I take Squib into the house. Squib runs into Bird's arms with a swirl of blond pigtails.

"Are you going to Uncle Tam's funeral?" I ask Amanda as we go to join Ranger.

"Yes, though I hate funerals," she says. "They're all black and you have to keep still forever and a week while everyone talks about the person you love and it's not really like them at all, except you hear about the weird things they did when they were young. And people gawk at you because you're the people who're sad . . ."

The three of us go up to the hay-loft where we pull and heave hay bales to build a fort. Amanda talks and talks. Then she looks at me and says, "You haven't said anything for ages. What're you thinking about?"

"Uncle Tam's dog, Sandy," I say.

Ranger's horrified face pops up above a hay bale.

Amanda says, "Why about Sandy? What's so special about him now?"

I pull hay out of my ponytail and say, "Er . . . have

you heard anything about him since Uncle Tam died?"

"My dad said he got swept down-river and drowned," says Amanda. "Though he could have been rescued and someone doesn't know who to call. Maybe he chased the Dakens' burglar all the way down to the road, and somebody found him and took him home with them."

"Maybe," Ranger says.

"We'll be a band of detectives. Maybe we can catch the burglar and find out how Uncle Tam died, and we'll be famous and get our photos in the papers. And we'll find Sandy and you'll be okay again, more or less."

Amanda goes on talking and talking.

Soon the old cowbell rings across the acreage to call us for lunch. Amanda shakes off the hay from her clothes. "I'd better go, Dad will have my lunch ready. We're going shopping this afternoon since I need new shoes. I've grown out of my runners and Sunday shoes and I want red runners with green laces. See you at school on Monday." She climbs the gate out of the barnyard, waves, and runs down the driveway.

Ranger and I go inside. Everyone is at the dining room table.

"Did you see The McGuire's dog?" Bird asks.

Ranger kicks me under the table and says, "The McGuire chased us off."

"The dog's behind his house. You can hear it, but you can't see it from the road," says Michael.

"When did he get it?" Bird asks.

"A couple of weeks ago," says Michael. "At least, that's when I first heard him."

"What happened to Uncle Tam's dog?" Bird asks.

"He vanished," says Ma. "No one's seen him since Tam died."

"I think he drowned in the river," Michael says.

I don't want to say we've seen him over at The McGuire's place. Pa told us not to go there and when Pa or Ma tell us something we're supposed to listen. I finish my peanut butter and pickle sandwich. Squib dribbles a spoonful of soup on the floor, which Tucker licks up. I give Ranger a sharp look, in case he even thinks about telling Ma and Pa we were snooping around The McGuire place.

"Seth says he's been job-hunting," Pa says. "But he won't take anything until he's not needed at Tam's place."

"Seth will find himself a steady job and settle down one day." Ma sighs. "He's had more jobs than there are fleas on a dog."

"Why did you ask him to look after Uncle Tam's

place?" Bird asks. "He's not the most reliable guy around."

"He used to look after it when Tam was off in Alberta, so he knows the place," says Pa. " And we had to get someone there quickly."

Tucker sticks his head in my lap, and I scratch behind his ears. "Tucker doesn't have fleas," I say.

Ma takes a bite of her food. "I was over at Tam's place today and Seth asked if you were back for the funeral, Bird."

"He gives me the creeps," Bird says.

"How are Uncle Tam's cows?" I ask Ma.

"Other than that escape-artist calf, they're fine. Bessie is due to calve any day."

Right then the phone rings and Ranger answers it. He hands the phone to Bird. "It's Seth."

I hear her say, "No. Absolutely not. Goodbye." She hangs up and says, "Seth may know about horses but he's clueless about people. He wanted me to go out on a date tonight!" She passes me, without touching my shoulder, as she goes back to her chair. I'm sad: she's forgotten, grown away from me, since she's moved away.

Michael asks if he can take the car up to the auction up on the highway, where his girlfriend, Ellie, works.

Pa nods, and then says, "Frame, have you forgotten? It's your turn to muck out the barn."

"I'm supposed to help the Dakens clean the stables."

"Do your chores here first, Frame."

"Okay." I groan and grab my boots.

Outside a chill wind whips against my jacket, and I tighten the collar. The sky hangs low and grey, and it's starting to rain. The Dakens' horses are in the pasture, so I suppose I won't be needed today anyway.

I squeeze through the gate and grab a shovel.

It's still raining lightly when I take the last load to the manure pile, put the tools away, and climb up to the hayloft where Ranger is waiting for me. He's brought the cookie tin. We sit in the middle of the fort and start eating. It feels spooky in the scratchy dark. A dog barks in the distance.

I take another cookie. Crumbs spill down my shirt.

"I wonder why The McGuire doesn't want us to know he's got Sandy," I say.

"Weird that he has him tied up at the back."

"He doesn't know how to look after him," I say. "I don't like The McGuire."

"You haven't liked him since he chased us out of his yard when we tried to rescue one of his turkeys that got stuck in a tree," Ranger says.

I laugh, though I screamed and cried at the time.

"I had to rescue the turkey." I take the last cookie. "With Uncle Tam and The McGuire knowing each other, it makes a kind of sense that The McGuire would have Sandy be a guard dog after Uncle Tam died."

Ranger gets up and stretches.

I brush crumbs from my jacket. "I wish we had some clues about who killed Uncle Tam. The police haven't found anything yet; at least they've not said they have."

"I bet they've not looked in the right places. We could check along the river ourselves—the stretch above the bridge where it makes the border between Uncle Tam's farm and the Dakens'."

"We could hunt through the bushes."

"Good idea." Ranger stands up.

"We'll do some real detecting," I say. We grin at each other.

Ranger goes down the ladder and steps outside. I scramble after him, taking the empty cookie tin with me. Primrose is standing there, in the shelter of the barn, waiting for the other cows to join her.

The sky is clearing with blue patches showing through, as I splash through the yard and the garden.

The rest of the day goes by in a blur. With Bird

home, we all want a piece of her time. I hang around the kitchen and pick up what I can of her life in Victoria.

On Sunday morning, after a night of hard frost, Finch Dakens phones to ask if I'll ride Gypsy. I run across the fields to the stable and find Seth and a couple of other riders saddling up.

Seth says, "Hi, good day for a ride."

"Couldn't be better." I grin.

"How's school?"

"I failed my math test."

"Never mind," he says.

"It's the funeral on Tuesday."

"Yes. I know." Seth puts my saddle on Gypsy. I adjust the bridle and reins and lead Gypsy out. The riders gather along the fence with Finch by the gate to the trail. I'm in the middle of the group as we ride out, with Finch in the lead and Suzie at the end; she shuts the gate.

People talk back and forth round me, but I don't know what to say as I don't know them well. I keep Gypsy on a tight rein to slow her down. People pass me on a wide grassy area. I find myself riding with Seth whom I know a bit better than the others. Perhaps I can do some detecting? I stare at the trail between

Gypsy's ears; change the reins from one hand to the other. I'm not sure what to ask. Then, as Seth and I ride down the trail I have an idea.

"Have you heard anything about Sandy?" I ask.

"Not a word."

"Do you think he's alive somewhere?" I look sideways at him.

"I thought he drowned in the river."

"You don't think he was rescued downstream?" I twist the reins round my fingers. I feel awkward asking questions when I know where Sandy is, but I want to know what people think happened.

"I'm sure we'd have heard if he had."

"I think we should have had him at our place."

"Tucker and Sandy didn't get along."

"That's true . . . they snarled at each other." I chew the inside of my mouth. "But it'd make more sense, since Uncle Tam was our almost-uncle."

A pair of crows calls from the nearby trees. I watch one fly up and away toward the mountains, thinking of Uncle Tam. "You used to work for Uncle Tam, didn't you?"

"Off and on, looked after the place when he was away. Brice McGuire worked for him more than I did, hauling cattle to the auction or to buyers."

We ride through the woods, up the road, and back

into woods, the other riders strung out ahead and behind us.

"Has Bird said anything about me?" Seth asks. "I want to buy her a present."

"She has a boyfriend in Victoria. His name is Leo," I say, looking away. Bird may not like Seth but he seems okay to me.

He drops back and starts to talk with Suzie. I ride on listening to the clip of hooves against the hard trail. I imagine that I'm riding Midnight. The sunlight reminds me of Uncle Tam helping us bring in the hay last summer.

We get back to the stable around noon.

Seth takes Gypsy's saddle off and says, "I think you're wrong about Bird having a guy in Victoria. She's *my* girl." He grabs a pitchfork and thrusts it hard and fast into a bale of straw.

I reach for Gypsy's bridle and take it off, keeping away from Seth. He picks up his saddle and thumps it onto its peg, growling, breathing heavily. I hang the bridle on its peg then go and help Finch and Suzie brush down horses and muck out the stables.

Finch and Suzie do most of the wheelbarrow work. I shovel a lot of manure though.

CHAPTER 5

TUESDAY ROLLS AROUND WITH another hard frost overnight. The day of Uncle Tam's funeral. And I hate it. I don't like having to wear a skirt. And I hate having to sit up front where everyone can see me. I hate having all those people behind me. I hate swallowing the crying. I hate that it's Uncle Tam in the coffin right there in front of us. I hate that it's a black hard icy kind of day. And I really hate Uncle Tam being put into the ground with the dirt going plunk, plunk on the wood.

Afterward everyone eats and drinks and talks. Seth tries to glue himself to Bird, but she gives him a look that would freeze hot toast. I take a plate of food and hide behind the church hall. Ranger and Amanda find me; we eat together and don't say a word.

Then everyone leaves, even Bird. We go home to milk cows, feed chickens, and have soup for dinner. I'm tired: I wish Uncle Tam hadn't died. I go to bed and dream of black dresses. I wake up feeling relieved that the funeral is over.

It's a good thing it's Wednesday and the funeral is over. Ma makes pancakes for breakfast: I put large spoonfuls of yogurt and relish on my pancake and stir them together. A good start to the day.

Ranger finishes his pancakes and waits for me. Michael bangs the front door shut as he comes in, red-nosed and cold from milking Primrose. Ma hands him a coffee. Michael sits down with Tucker at his feet, pulls a dog-eared stamp catalogue from his pocket, and begins to read.

I gobble another pancake, grab my jacket and school bag, and head out the door. Ma blows a kiss. She looks tired.

I leave with Ranger and, before we get to the end of the driveway, say, "Let's play hooky, we've got detecting to do. And if we discover who the murderer is, no one will care that we skipped school."

He doesn't need convincing.

Ranger follows me. We stuff our back-packs under the bushes by the driveway and walk up the hill. The cows stare, chewing.

"First let's look along the river. I bet we'll find clues there," Ranger says.

"I don't want to go below the bridge where we found Uncle Tam," I say.

"The police have searched all over there anyway."

"Let's look up river instead, between Uncle Tam's place and the Dakens'."

A flock of starlings surges up from the telephone lines into the blue-as-summer sky. They whirl away.

All of a sudden we hear Tucker bark. He scoots under a fence onto the road right beside us, and jumps up and down.

"Michael should have put him in his run," I say.

"Never mind. Let's go."

We go down to the lookout just past Amanda's place, with Tucker foraging ahead of us. The grass is white with frost and crackles underfoot.

"Did you hear The McGuire yelling at Sandy last night?" I ask as we slide and scramble down the bank.

"Couldn't miss it."

I slip the last few yards on my backside. There's bracken, brown and dead, under the trees along the river. There's frost on the trees. It covers the ground, crinkled and thin. I like the feel of the prickling ferns and the way shrubs pull at my hair and clothes. I imagine riding down here on Midnight. A pair of chickadees flits away to one side.

Ranger, Tucker and I work our way along the bank, up-river from the bridge and through the trees, which stand spooky and dark. Tucker disappears ahead of us.

I pick up two cigarette butts. "They might have been dropped by the murderer."

Ranger finds a torn plastic bag and tosses it away. I pick it up and put the butt ends from my pocket in it, then put it in one of my pockets.

"Do you think they're clues?" Ranger asks.

"They might be, but also they could be swallowed by a deer and it'd get sick and die."

"You can't save every animal on the planet, Frame."

"I can try."

We scramble through brambles, over old tree trunks and round bends. The river runs fast beside us, down toward the bridge.

I remember the day we found Uncle Tam. I shiver; my hands are cold. There's ice on the protected cove where we swim in summer. Tucker appears, nose to the ground, tail in the air, perhaps on the trail of a rabbit.

I find a mint wrapper above the cove, more cigarette butts, and a bottle cap; but no murderer's tracks. I put everything in the plastic bag in my pocket which is beginning to bulge. Tucker rejoins us, his tongue hanging out.

"Look over there," I say to Ranger, pointing at the opposite side of the river, Uncle Tam's side. Broken and crushed willow-shrubs bend into the water among torn brambles. I half expect a villain to leap out of the trees.

The bank behind us has a long, gentle grade up to the Dakens' house, the firs and maples widely spaced. We work our way across the slope, searching for clues. I pick up another mint wrapper and find a place where someone slipped a few feet. Ranger says it could have been one of the Dakens.

"Let's go over to Uncle Tam's side," says Ranger.

"Sure."

Ranger heads up-river to the old foot-bridge; Tucker and I follow. Two huge fifty-foot trees were felled years ago to lie tight together across the river. A narrow path leads up to Uncle Tam's barns on the other side. It's tricky and a bit scary crossing, so we go gingerly, the water rushing beneath us. Tucker stays on Dakens' side and watches us.

We pause at the foot of the path toward the barns, the ground frozen hard under our feet. The shrubs and brambles are torn and tangled. We stand in silence. What was Uncle Tam doing here? I look up-river, then across to the Dakens', then down-river where the water curls round the tiny spit of land that holds the cove. I wonder what, or who, Uncle Tam saw.

Ranger walks up the path toward the barns, examining the ground.

"Let's see what we can find in the bushes," I call. "You go up-river from here, and I'll go down toward the road."

I get caught on brambles as I trample down saplings, thrust bushes out of my way, wriggle through dense growth, trip on salal, then fall against an alder.

"There's nothing here!" I yell.

"There's just frozen mud here!" Ranger shouts.

A bramble scrapes the back of my hand and I lick the trickle of blood. I scramble through the bushes. Then my foot slips on the bank. I grab for a tree to keep from falling, but catch a bramble instead and land with my face in the dirt.

"Ouch! And more ouch!" I pull a thorn from the palm of my hand, suck the blood, and imagine a bear or a cougar sniffing along my blood-trail. I wriggle round and sit up, feet hanging over the bank, back against a young tree. I take a deep breath and watch the river. Tucker would protect me from wild animals.

A strand of what looks like blond horsehair, caught on a twig bending into the water, trembles in the wind. It might be a clue. I go flat on my stomach and edge out over the river to reach it. With one hand under the lip of the bank to steady myself, I stretch forward and catch the hair. But it isn't a length of horsehair, it's a single strand from a length of rope.

I wind it round my fingers, pull it straight, and consider it. It must have come from up-river. I put it in another pocket and turn back to follow the edge of the bank. I squirm under the shrubs until at last, with my hair snarled in twigs, I see a length of rope, streaming out close to the surface. I pull my hair free, which hurts. I reach for the partly unravelled rope, get hold of it, but I can't free it, no matter how much I tug and yank. It's too tightly tangled.

I skid back onto firm ground and yell, "Ranger, come and see."

He yells back, then I hear him whacking and bashing his way through the trees and undergrowth. He joins me, a short stick in one hand. I hold the end of the rope out of the water and look at it.

"I can't get it out. See how it's caught under the surface, maybe in some roots, under the curve of the bank?" I show him. "And see the end, how it looks as if it's been cut?"

"It's a funny place for a bit of rope," Ranger says.

I stand up. "Weird."

Tucker barks on the other bank.

I'm afraid of what Tucker has found. Leaving the rope, I turn quickly, fight, push, and struggle through the shrubs, to the path and then across the footbridge to Dakens' side. There, Ranger on my heels, I dodge trees, scrambling down-river to the cove and the frozen-over pool where we swim in summer.

"Slow down!" Ranger shouts behind me.

The current swirls in swift eddies on the far side, Uncle Tam's side, where we swim. There's nobody there, nothing at all. Maybe a deer or a rabbit took off when it saw Tucker?

He goes out on the ice a few steps, still barking. I laugh as he slithers and slides.

Ranger follows. The ice cracks. And there's Ranger, sitting on his butt, cold water slopping at his thighs, with Tucker bouncing over him back to shore. Tucker shakes the water from his fur.

I laugh and laugh.

Then Ranger stands up: his right hand drips blood.

CHAPTER 6

I CHOKE AND ALMOST VOMIT. GASPING for breath, I wade into the water and grab Ranger by the arm—he just stands there and stares at the blood. I see a gleam of metal among the rocks, under the surface. I drag him to the bank. Scarlet drops drip down from his hand. There's a great slash across it. I try to think clearly.

"Is it glass? Is it stuck in your hand?"

Ranger stands and stares at the blood welling across his palm.

I toss my jacket onto the bank. "We need to bandage that and get help." I pull my outer shirt over my head and tie it round his hand. My hands shake so badly I can hardly tie the knot. Tucker jumps up and Ranger pushes him away. He holds his hand high, blood seeping through my shirt and sliding down his wrist.

"Wait here," I say, pushing him down onto a log. I wade back toward the rocks where Ranger fell and look into the water. Broken ice swirls away in the current. There it is. I reach in carefully, slide my fingers round it, and pull out a knife. Its blade is open. It's Uncle Tam's knife, his farmer's knife. I close the blade, put the knife in my pocket.

Then, freezing and scared, I pull myself up the bank and shrug myself into my jacket. Ranger stands and carefully we start up the path, Tucker at our heels. Ranger stops, holds onto a sapling with his good hand for a minute, then continues, one slow step at a time.

We stop and I bang on the Dakens' door, but no one's home. The horses move away as we cut across the fields. Ranger's face is pale, grey and green. He's walking very slowly.

I run, fast as I can. Tucker leaps beside me. The chickens scatter as I sprint through the yard, yelling for Ma. I burst into the kitchen. Ma's sitting at the table, drinking coffee, with Squib on her knee.

"It's Ranger . . . he's cut his hand. There's blood everywhere." I blurt out as he stumbles in behind me.

Ma jumps up, pushing Squib to the floor all in one movement, and heads out the door.

"And I found Uncle Tam's knife!" I shout. She doesn't hear me. I stand there, gasping for breath, not sure what to do.

Ma comes in with Ranger. "Frame, get me some

ice and a few clean towels."

I grab dish towels and a pack of frozen peas and hand them to Ma.

"Get changed, Frame," Ma says as she wraps up his hand, "and get dry clothes for Ranger as well."

Upstairs I find track pants, dry socks and a sweatshirt for Ranger. I change, rush downstairs and hand Ranger's clothes to Ma.

"Ranger, get changed," she says. "Frame, take Squib out to the car."

I scoop Squib and Bear from the kitchen floor. We race outside and scramble into the car, with me and Squib in the back. In no time at all Ranger gets in up front with Ma.

"He needs stitches," says Ma, as she pulls out of the driveway. "You kids! What on earth were you doing?"

My voice comes out in a squeak. "Playing hooky."

Ma sounds as if she has ice chips between her teeth. "When will the pair of you get your brains in order and stop skipping school?"

"We were looking for clues ..." Ranger says.

". . . along the river below the Dakens' place," I continue.

"And did I hear you say you'd found Uncle Tam's knife, Frame?" Ma asks.

"Yes, it was in the rocks."

Ranger gasps. "What? That must have been what cut my hand."

I pull the knife out of my pocket and hold it over the seat back between Ma and Ranger.

"Holy jumping jacks!" Ranger says.

Ma glances at it. "Yes, that's Tam's knife, for sure." She takes it from me and shoves it into her jacket pocket.

She bangs her fist on the steering wheel. "You two should have more sense than to go down by the river in winter. Let the police look for clues, it's their job."

I chew my lower lip. "We were trying to help solve Uncle Tam's murder," I say.

"We don't know where—or if—Uncle Tam was murdered . . . It's not a game, so leave detecting to those who know how." She bangs the steering wheel again. She drives fast. "Stupid place to be . . . stupid thing to do," she mutters over and over.

Ranger rests his head against the back of the seat.

Squib cuddles up to me, tucks her head under my arm and sucks her thumb. Being Squib seems so easy: all she needs is someone to hold her.

Ma parks at the hospital and hurries in with Ranger. I follow with Squib hanging onto me, Bear dangling from her other hand. We sit in the waiting room and watch people come and go.

Eventually, Ma comes out of the nursing area and makes a few calls. Then she sits down beside me and takes Squib on her knee.

"I called the schools to say you were all home sick today."

"Will Ranger be okay?"

"They're stitching him up. He'll have a scar, but he'll be fine." Ma bounces Squib up and down and Squib gurgles and dribbles.

She turns and frowns at me. "Don't you ever skip school again."

"Never." I lean against her, rubbing my head against her arm. She smells of wool, soap and coffee. My stomach rumbles.

"I'd like to whale the living daylight out of the pair of you." She sighs heavily. Ma sounds disconnected and strange. She stares into space for a minute. My tummy rumbles again. She reaches, absent-mindedly, into her pocket. "Here's change for the vending machine."

I get some chips, and we share them.

Ranger comes back with the doctor. Ranger's face looks like a dirty sheet and his hand is a huge bundle of white bandages. He sits down.

I relax and move close to Ranger. "How many stitches?"

"Four," he says.

Squib touches his bandaged hand with a pokey finger.

"Squib, don't touch." Ma brings Squib close to her. She leans against Ma and stares at Ranger's hand.

The doctor says, "Ranger should see his own doctor to have the stitches out, in ten days' time. If the cut gets inflamed or sore in anyway, take him in right away."

"Okay," says Ma.

Squib takes a quick swipe at Ranger's hand with Bear. "Bear wants a big white paw."

Ma catches Squib's other hand. "Squib, don't touch, I mean it. Ranger's hand is very sore."

"Bear wants stitches *and* a big white paw," Squib insists.

"Okay," says Ma. "When we get home, Bear can have a bandage."

The doctor says, "And, Ranger, no more walking on thin ice!" He pats Ranger's shoulder before turning back to deal with the next patient. We go back out to the car.

Ma starts the engine, then she pauses. "I'll call the police when we get home, let them know we've found Tam's knife."

"The police?" I ask.

"Does that mean they'll want to talk to me?" Ranger's eyes spread wide, and he goes pink in the face. I look at his sling and the fat bandage on his hand. Ranger will be a hero at school.

I offer him the last of the chips.

On the way home, Ma says, "Frame, you get to do Ranger's chores until his hand heals."

"Tack-spit and pignuts!"

"He gets the cut hand for being stupid, you get extra chores; that's fair."

I grumble quietly to Squib. She smiles round her thumb.

CHAPTER 7

WHEN WE ARRIVE HOME, MA CALLS the police, and explains that we have found Uncle Tam's knife.

Ma says, "They'll be here shortly as they are just up at the auction."

Ranger goes up to his room. I hang my jacket in the cupboard and go down to the rec room with Squib.

It was supposed to be an ordinary day, playing hooky, looking for clues, but it's all gone wrong and we have to talk to the police. I help Squib build block towers and knock them down. I don't like talking to people I don't know.

I hear knocking on the front door and Ma opening it. She calls Ranger and me to the kitchen. Squib trails up after me, cuddling Bear.

There are two police officers, one leaning against the counter while the other stands with a notebook in his hand.

Ma introduces Ranger and me, ruffles my hair,

and says, "Tell the officers what happened and where you were." And she goes back to making lunch.

My heart hits my boots. Couldn't Ma have told them? Couldn't Ranger do it? Ma smiles at me from the kitchen. I rub one foot up and down my leg, push Squib in front of me, and look at the floor. The officers wear black shoes; one pair has mud around the toes. The other pair has laces done up crookedly.

"We went up the river . . . the Koksilah . . . at Cowichan Station . . . Ranger fell through the ice . . . and cut his hand." I can't think of anything else to say.

Muddy-shoe moves one foot slightly. "I grew up near Kelowna . . . used to play hooky to fish in a local creek," he says.

I hold Squib closer and study the pattern on the floor.

Muddy Shoe makes notes then says to Ranger, "You got yourself a bad cut, I understand. It must hurt a lot. But can you just tell us exactly where you fell in the river?"

Ranger describes Dakens' pool. Crooked Lace says he used to swim there when he was growing up.

"My sister found some clues," Ranger says. "We were trying to solve Uncle Tam's murder."

Muddy Shoe says, "What did you find?"

Ranger nudges me. I slither round the officers and fetch the plastic bag with the mint wrappers and cigarette butts from the pocket of my jacket. I hold them out, without looking up.

Muddy Shoe takes them with a muttered "Oh . . . thanks." He doesn't sound impressed or interested.

Squib announces, "Bear is going to have a big fat white paw, like Ranger."

Crooked Lace laughs and says, "Good idea."

Ma says, "We'll fix his paw after lunch, Squib."

I'm happy Squib interrupted: I don't want to be even more embarrassed by giving Muddy Shoe the strand of rope, and having to explain about it.

Crooked Lace asks if there was anyone around.

"The Dakens were out," I mutter, half-hiding behind Ranger.

"We'll phone and go up there later," Crooked Lace says.

"Why does it matter?" Ranger asks.

"It might contribute to an ongoing investigation," Muddy Shoe says.

"You mean Uncle Tam's knife might be the one that killed him?" Ranger gasps.

"There are other cases we're working on too," says Crooked Lace. "But, Mrs. Williams, if you would let us have the knife, please?"

Ma gives it to him, saying, "You will let us have it back though, won't you?"

"That may not be possible," says Muddy Shoe. "I'll see what I can do."

Ma offers them lunch, but they refuse and leave. I nibble at the edge of a sandwich; I'm not hungry. Ranger doesn't eat much either.

Afterward, he goes to his room. I follow, sit on the edge of the bed, and chew my ponytail. I stare out the window, pull my feet up and sit cross-legged.

I twist my hair. "I didn't tell them about the rope, and that single strand was in another pocket, not with the butts and stuff."

"It looked like a collection of litter you'd picked up along the road."

"They'll probably chuck it away." I watch Ranger wriggle the fingers of his cut hand. "We can always tell them about the rope later . . ."

". . . or we can find the other end ourselves?"

"I suppose so." I pull my ponytail. "I wonder if whoever robbed the Dakens killed Uncle Tam."

Ranger cradles his cut hand in the other hand. "The burglary and Uncle Tam's death have to be connected."

"I think so, too." I think hard. "But I wonder how the burglar got hold of the knife."

"Maybe Uncle Tam dropped the knife when he was running away from the thief?" Ranger says.

"Or the thief picked it up, caught up with Uncle Tam, and . . ."

". . . stabbed him," Ranger finishes.

I don't want to go on imagining. I can see it all in my head; I can see blood and danger. Ranger picks at his bandage.

I chew my ponytail, then say, "Do you think we should tell the police about Sandy?"

"That's not connected . . . It's our mystery, and we'll find the answer," Ranger says.

"We need to rescue Sandy before he dies of starvation."

I stand up, go to the dining room and spread my homework over the table. But the knife comes between me and the books. Did The McGuire kill Uncle Tam? Why else would he have Sandy?

It's Saturday morning. I get dressed and fix my ponytail. The house is quiet and the kitchen empty. I make a milkshake with an egg, milk, banana and chocolate milk mix.

Ranger comes down while I'm making toast. He takes a piece. Ma and Squib come up from the basement. Pa comes in the front door and kicks his boots into the kitchen cupboard.

"Primrose got her head through the fence and ate the new raspberry shoots," he grumbles. "I'll have to fix the hole."

Ranger whispers, "Let's go and rescue Sandy."

"I'll get my pocket knife to cut the rope," I say.

We go outside into the cold. Ranger rubs his nose with the back of his hand. The scar on his hand is still red and raw after ten days. I remember the blood dripping from it and shiver.

"We'd better check to see if The McGuire's truck is in before we sneak around back."

We go down the road and past The McGuire's place. There's no truck. I take out my pocket knife.

Just then a truck comes past us and we move to the edge of the road. Then there's another truck. It's The McGuire.

Sandy barks from behind the house. As he gets out of his truck, The McGuire shouts, "Shut up, dog!"

I kick gravel and put my knife back in my pocket.

The McGuire shouts, "Hey, you kids, want to make some money? I need my turkey barn shovelled out."

"No," I whisper to Ranger, "no way."

"Give you five bucks each," The McGuire shouts.

"Five bucks, Frame. I need the money," Ranger says. He's saving for another Bruce Springsteen tape.

"No," I say. "No way."

Ranger ignores me and shouts at The McGuire, "Okay, we'll do it."

"Traitor," I hiss. "Spinach-head. Pig-butt."

There's a brief silence, then The McGuire shouts, "Come and grab a pitchfork."

Ranger whispers, "We can snoop for clues."

Stubborn as Pa, he walks down the road to The McGuire's driveway. I follow. Sandy barks again.

One foot moves in front of the other and my legs take me into The McGuire's line of sight.

He stands in front of his house, a run-down stucco one-storey building.

"That shed." He points to one next door to one the turkeys are using. "It needs cleaning out, and there's the wheelbarrow, shovels and pitchforks."

"Where do we put the crap and stuff?" Ranger asks. I notice he says "we": he knows I'll join him. I'd rather hit him.

The McGuire thumbs toward the back of the house. He stares at us for a minute, then says, "I'll put the dog in my workshop. He bites."

I come up to Ranger's left, behind his shoulder, away from The McGuire. "Er . . . can I take your dog for a walk sometime?"

"Don't go near my dog. He's a guard dog," The

McGuire says. He sits down on the step and pops the top off a bottle of beer.

I open the door of the turkey shed to be met by a wall of stench.

"Whew!" I gag and hold my nose.

"Breathe through your mouth," says Ranger.

"Breathe through your ears, you idiot. This is the hugest, most revolting, stinking idea you ever had." I turn and hiss in his face. "You're a stubborn, flea-bitten cabbage face!"

Ranger grins. "We'll earn some money."

I stick my tongue out at him.

Ranger grabs a shovel and digs into the muck. His mouth is open and he gulps air as he dumps a load into the barrow. I take it round the side of the house, past tarp-covered boxes and the old freezers, to the compost.

I go back to the shed and shovel more sludge, gagging in the stink.

"Ranger, do dead bodies smell?" I ask, leaning on my shovel.

"They must," he answers. "And they turn green and yellow too."

We take turns with the wheelbarrow. Ranger says he's snooping into boxes and crates when he's round the back. "Have to be quick though."

On my next turn, I open an ancient freezer behind the house, curious to see what's inside. I lift a few squashed boxes and stand there, stunned. I can't believe it: the Dakens' gold coins lie half-covered by an old newspaper. I shut the lid quickly and carefully, afraid The McGuire will catch me.

I go back to the turkey shed and whisper, "Ranger, the Dakens' gold coins are in the freezer."

"The McGuire's the thief," Ranger whispers. "We should tell the police."

"No, he'll know it's us that told. He'll kill us."

Next time I'm round the back, I run for the workshop, open the door, and Sandy is there, tied to a work-bench. His bones stick out and his coat is matted and dirty. I itch to cut him free. He is a shrunken version of Uncle Tam's healthy Sandy. I crouch down and rub his head. He licks my hand and snuggles against me.

I gulp, sniff and wipe my nose on my arm.

"Oh *Sandy*," I whisper. I hug him, stand up, and leave, closing the door quietly behind me. What am I going to do? I tell Ranger and he's shocked.

"We can't do anything right here and now," he says. Ranger takes another load to the pile.

I keep shovelling, then there's an awful crash behind the house.

The McGuire jumps up and, swearing loudly, rushes off. He comes back, dragging Ranger by one ear. "You get off my property and don't ever come back, you sneaking, snooping, boil-brained louts. You steaming fumets," he roars.

He runs Ranger down to the road, swearing all the way.

I dump tools and follow.

"You can have two dollars and that's it for the weaselling little maggot that you are," The McGuire shouts. He holds out a two dollar bill and I snatch it as I run past. "Snooping round my yard . . ."

I catch up with Ranger. "What were you doing?"

"Poking in a pile of crates. They fell over." He rubs his ear. "And there was nothing interesting there, just junk." He shakes his head. "I like 'boil-brained', though, that's a good swear."

"What's a fumet?"

"Deer crap."

"Oh . . . well, never mind," I say. "We found the coins, and I talked to Sandy. Though we can't go there again when The McGuire's around."

I'm angry with Ranger for getting us into this, never mind the money.

"We learned something and got paid to do it," Ranger says.

I lean my face close to his. "I was scared. He's weird, and we shouldn't have been there."

"He didn't like us asking about Sandy," says Ranger.

"Let's rescue him tonight."

"Tomorrow night; there's a hockey double-header on TV tonight," Ranger says. "I'll be watching it with Pa and Ma."

"Tomorrow night, then," I say, "We could grab the coins too."

"If you say so." Ranger pokes my shoulder.

"We live across the road from a murderer." I shiver at the idea.

"He must have grabbed Sandy after he killed Uncle Tam," says Ranger.

I take off at full speed, my hair pulled by the wind, like galloping on horseback. Ranger passes me but stops on our driveway. I bump into him, knock him down, jump on him and pummel him as hard as I can. "That's for getting us into turkey stink."

Ranger slithers out from under me, stands up and puts a headlock on me.

Then Bird calls, "Hi, you two!"

I turn and run down the driveway, shouting, "Bird! You're home!"

Pa and Ma are leaning against the truck in the sun, eating chips. Squib sits on the grass, holding Bear, and sings, "Chip slip pip," over and over again. The truck's hood is up and there are tools on the ground. Bird comes toward me.

I want to hug her but, when I get close, she says, "What in the world have you been doing? You stink!"

"We cleaned out The McGuire's turkey barn."

"I told you not to go to his place," Pa says.

"He asked us to do it," Ranger says.

Ma offers me the chips.

I shrug and take a few; Ranger takes a handful.

"Frame, you and Ranger stay off his property," Pa says. "It's the last time I'm telling you."

"Yes, Pa," I mutter, digging my toes into the dirt.

I narrow my eyes at Ranger, pull my lips tight together, and shake my head, warning him in my mind not to say anything about the gold coins or Sandy.

"You two, go take a shower and change clothes. Don't touch anything until you're clean," Ma says.

"Leave your boots outside," Pa shouts after us.

There's a hose attached by the front door so I pick up the end and take it down to the driveway. Ranger turns the tap on and I begin to wash my boots. Then I turn the hose on Ranger and hit him in the chest.

He ducks out of the cold water, sticks his tongue out at me, and grins. I soak him some more, then turn the hose away.

He thumps me as he goes by and says, "I don't have to shower now."

"You do! You still stink."

I make a face at him, put the hose away and go inside. Ranger is in the shower so I have to wait. When I'm dressed, I go out and watch the cows. The maples and firs along the creek bend with the wind, and there are patches of sunlight on the fields.

CHAPTER 8

I FEEL FRUSTRATED: THERE'S NOTHING I can do except have lunch. I slide into a chair beside Ranger, poke him, and whisper, "I'm worried that The McGuire will move the coins."

"He doesn't know we've seen them."

"That's true." I eat my peanut butter and tomato sandwich and plan how to rescue Sandy.

After lunch, Bird takes Squib on her knee and sings to her. I go to the sitting room, where *The Incredible Journey* lies on the coffee-table. I lie on my stomach on the floor and go on reading. But the words have no meaning: I'm seeing Sandy, his matted fur, bald neck.

The front door bangs, and I hear Pa calling Ranger and me. I go to the kitchen.

"I had a chat with Mr. McGuire, and he gave me $5 to give you for cleaning up his turkey shed," he tells us, handing us $2.50 each. "He says you did a good job."

"He didn't say anything else?" asks Ranger.

"What else would he say?" Pa eyes us suspiciously.

"Nothing," I say, giving Ranger a stern look.

"He's a strange man . . . in the Navy for twenty years . . . Don't go snooping around his property again, ever."

Pa's not mad at us so I relax and go on reading. Later in the day I manage to steal some time with Bird. She tells me about her Economics professor and a show she went to with Leo.

"Stephie put gum in my hair," I interrupt.

"How did you get it out?"

"I pulled and clawed it out, really," I say.

"Leo's kitten clawed my blue sweater when I was over there the other day," Bird says.

"How old is the kitten?"

"He's so cute, he's three month's old. He sits on Leo's knee when he's studying, and plays with his pens."

I'm tired of hearing about Leo. Bird talks about him and university all the time. She's moved into another world and doesn't share mine the way she used to.

Michael comes home in time for dinner. He was out at the auction helping Ellie. "Mr. McGuire came to the auction today," he says, putting a slice of meatloaf and a glob of potatoes on his plate.

"Did he have a dog with him?" Ranger asks.

Squib puts her carrots on my plate; I put them back on hers.

"In his truck, he said; I didn't see him." Michael eats meatloaf and beans.

"What else did he say?" I wish meatloaf didn't look like the inside of a compost heap.

"He told me he needs a guard dog to keep mink and people away from his birds."

"It isn't going to keep mink away if it's tied up all the time," says Bird.

"Behind his house, too," says Ranger.

Squib's carrots arrive back on my plate.

I poke my slice of meatloaf and say, "The McGuire is not a nice person at all."

"Just because you think he doesn't look after his dog doesn't mean he's bad," Bird says.

"A good person looks after dogs properly," I say.

Ranger joins Ma and Pa watching hockey downstairs. I hang around as long as I can but they're settled in for the evening. We're not going to be able to sneak out and rescue Sandy tonight.

It's Sunday morning, and big fat clouds billow across the sky like giant elephants. Ma makes pancakes and I have four, with yogurt and pickle on them.

The phone rings just as I'm wondering if I can manage another pancake. Ma takes the call, hangs up and says, "Frame, Ranger, that was Pa. He's over at Uncle Tam's place, and he says that one of the cows, Bessie, is calving. He thought you'd like to watch. She should calve in about an hour, he thinks."

"We'd better get going," I say. Our cows always seem to calve in the woods or down by the creek so we don't often get to watch.

Ranger gobbles his fifth pancake. He likes his with jam.

We put dishes in the sink, grab jackets and leave at the run. The wind blows hard, making our jackets blow out behind us.

Ranger pushes his hair out of his eyes, and I notice the scar.

I pull my jacket down and do it up.

We jog down the hill, run up Koksilah Road, turn before the railway bridge and arrive in Uncle Tam's yard out of breath.

We go to the big barns beyond the house. Ranger yells for Pa and he comes to the barn door.

"You're in time. Be quiet though," he says. "The calf's almost born. Bessie's having an easy time of it." He goes back into the barn and we follow.

Pa, Seth, Ranger and I lean on the rails of the

pen and watch Bessie's heaving flanks, and the push of her body. The calf's forelegs and head slide out, wrapped in a glistening sac. The body and back legs slip out smoothly.

Bessie turns and licks the calf, taking the sac and eating it. The calf puts one and then both forelegs under him, and staggers to his feet. Bessie licks and licks him, while he finds her udder, butts and pushes, and begins to suck. The afterbirth, large and dark red, slides from her body, and Bessie eats that too.

"Looks easy, doesn't it?" Pa says.

"It's so . . . so amazing," I say.

"Messy," says Ranger.

"Since you guys are here, you could help with chores," Seth says.

"Good idea," says Pa.

"Okay," I say. We might have the chance to do some detecting while we're here.

We help Pa herd cattle from one pasture to another. Then he and Seth start to shift hay bales. Pa asks us to muck out the barn. Maybe I'll spend my entire life shovelling manure out of barns. Again, Ranger and I take turns to shovel or empty the wheelbarrow.

Every chance I get, I lean on the rails and watch Bessie and her new calf, who is sleeping now.

As I'm taking yet another wheelbarrow load out,

I notice some rope halters hanging by the barn door, their ends grazing the floor. One rope is shorter than the others. I look at it closely: the end is cut. I lift it up. There are two small cuts beside the nose-band. I run my fingers down the lie of the rope and remember the piece stuck under the bank in the river, opposite the Dakens' house.

"Ranger, look at this," I say.

He sees the cut end and agrees it might be the other end of the rope we found.

"It could be the rope for the halter from Uncle Tam's escape-artist calf," I say.

"Seth found that calf in the woods at the end of Uncle Tam's property."

"Then I bet it had this halter on when Uncle Tam died," I say.

The calf must have got caught in the river. I picture the darkness, the calf thrashing, the halter knotted and tangled in the bushes. I can see Uncle Tam coming down the path, bending over the calf, calming it, getting his knife out to free the struggling calf.

"He saw the burglar," Ranger says, "or the burglar saw him from across the river and came and grabbed Uncle Tam's knife."

"So The McGuire killed Uncle Tam," I say, "because

Uncle Tam saw him stealing the coins." I pull the halter out straight. "We have to hide this halter." I pause and add, "So The McGuire can't come and get rid of it."

"He'll get rid of the coins soon, for sure."

"I'll hide it for now; we can tell the police about it later." I scramble up into the hay-loft and hide the halter right at the back behind the bales. Ranger goes to help Pa spread clean straw in a loose-box at the other end of the barn.

I slither down the ladder and wander over to watch Bessie and her calf.

Pa calls out, "We'll go home when this is done, Frame."

Then Seth comes in from across the yard with a couple of dollar bills in his hand. I hope he didn't hear me up in the hay loft. I glance at him, dig my hands into my pockets, try to look innocent and gaze at the calf.

Seth leans on the rail beside me.

I twist one foot behind the other: I mustn't give away any secrets even though The McGuire, the gold coins and the cut rope spin in my head.

"What's up?"

I wish I were as good as Ranger at thinking up fibs. I have to say something quickly. I blurt out,

"Seth, what would you do if a friend found something you knew had been stolen?"

He takes a step away from me. "Er . . . want to tell me about it?"

I shouldn't have said anything: Ranger and I aren't going to tell anyone. I manage to say, "I should talk to my friend about it first."

"Maybe I can help." He pauses for a long minute as if he expects me to say more. I hope I didn't give anything away. Ranger comes towards me.

Seth hands us a dollar each, saying, "Here's for this morning."

"Thanks," Ranger and I say together.

Pa joins us and sees the money. "That's good of you, Seth."

Seth shrugs, and Pa says it's time we went home for lunch.

Ranger gets into the back of the car and practises knots for Scouts. I slide into the front seat and watch the road without seeing it, as Pa drives up the hill past the lookout. I wonder if we have enough evidence to tell the police about The McGuire, the coins and the rope.

The smell of hamburgers greets us as we go in the house. Michael slices tomatoes while Ma flips burgers onto buns, hands them to us, and says, "Take them to the dining room, you two."

Ma, Pa and Squib get burgers too, and then Michael joins us. He piles onions, tomatoes and pickles on his burger. I have two, with cheese and relish, and finish up with an ice-cream cone.

"Have the police found any new clues about how Uncle Tam died?" I ask, trying to sound casual.

"They've not told us anything," says Ma.

"Nothing about the burglary either?" Ranger asks.

"Not a word," says Pa.

Bird says, "Seth called, it must have been just after you left Uncle Tam's place, and asked me to go to a movie with him tonight."

"Are you going?" Ma asks.

"No," says Bird.

"Remember when we had to change the pump last year and Seth came with Tam to help?" says Ma.

"And we all got covered with mud!" Pa laughs. "One of the joys of having a well dug in sticky clay soil!"

"You looked like hippos," I say, and laugh.

Ranger eats and eats. I wish he'd hurry up.

Michael asks if he can take the car for the rest of the day; he's taking Ellie out. When Ranger finishes, I jump up, leave my dishes in the sink, and say, "To the hayloft . . . let's go."

I shove my arms into the sleeves of my jacket as we race across the yard to the barns. Ranger climbs the ladder ahead of me. We tumble into the hayloft and huddle in amongst the bales.

It's a good thing Ma and Pa don't know we're going to rescue Sandy tonight. If it's dark enough, if Sandy doesn't bark, if The McGuire is out or asleep, if . . .

CHAPTER 9

I TELL RANGER HOW I'D ASKED SETH what a friend should do if they found something that had been stolen. "I hope he doesn't tell The McGuire what I said."

"We'll check if the coins are still there when we get Sandy," says Ranger.

"Tonight's the night." I chew my ponytail. "The knife is still a puzzle. How did it end up in the river? Could someone—The McGuire—kill Uncle Tam with his own knife?"

"We don't actually know that he was killed with a knife, you know." Ranger ties knots with a piece of string, while I pull hay from my hair.

"I think Uncle Tam went down to the river to free the calf and saw The McGuire sneaking around the Dakens' place. Then The McGuire saw him, crossed the river, got the knife from Uncle Tam and—and they fought for the knife and Uncle Tam died."

"Then he threw the knife in the river." Ranger

83

scratches the scar across the palm of his hand.

"What should we tell the police?" I spit out a wisp of hay.

"We could tell them about the coins," Ranger says. "Those are evidence."

I rub my hands over the hay. "But if they know where the coins are, they'll wonder why The McGuire keeps Sandy in his yard..."

"... And says nothing about him," Ranger interrupts.

"And I don't think we should tell them about the rope."

"Why not?"

"Because the cut end shows where Uncle Tam was along the river."

Ranger stares at the wall. "And that he must have seen The McGuire leaving the Dakens' after the break-in."

I pull hay from my socks. "If we tell the police about the coins or the rope, they'll go and question The McGuire..."

"... And The McGuire will decide he needs to get rid of Sandy because he ties The McGuire to the crime," Ranger finishes the sentence.

"Then we *must* rescue Sandy before we tell the police *any*thing," I say. "Sandy comes first!"

"I agree, and the sooner we get him the better."

He jumps up, goes down the ladder and I follow. Ranger goes to help Pa. I go to my bedroom, curl up on my bed, and dream of Sandy's rescue. Dinah curls up beside me, purring.

After dinner, I wander into the sitting room, watch the sun go down, stars begin to show, and the waning moon comes up. I have to stay awake late tonight. In the middle of a yawn I hear Michael come back from his date and go upstairs.

Next thing I know, Dinah wakes me by jumping on my chest. I sit up with a jerk. Ranger pokes me and says, "Everyone's asleep. Tucker's in with Michael."

I get up, stretch, and follow Ranger. Dinah's eyes gleam from the shadows when I look back over my shoulder.

"Let's go," I whisper, grabbing Bird's old red jacket to keep me warm.

We creep through the basement. The floor is concrete, so it doesn't creak.

I hold my breath as we sneak through the garage out into the open. I'm expecting Ma or Pa to shout at us. But all the windows are dark.

We walk on the grass along the edge of the driveway; a breeze lifts my hair across my eyes. I drag it back, twist it and stuff it inside my jacket, nervous and excited. The moon gives enough light for us to run down the road.

I stop under the trees at the corner and Ranger bumps into me.

"There's somebody there," I say.

The McGuire's truck is his driveway. I can see The McGuire in the bright moonlight. He is swinging boxes and crates from the truck-bed and carrying them round behind the house.

Ranger whispers over his shoulder, "There might be more stolen loot in those boxes."

Ranger creeps forward and I follow unhappily: The McGuire might run us down with his truck.

Ranger melts into the bushes at the end of the driveway; I follow him closely. We slip from shadow to shadow, from shrubs to piled junk. My heart thuds loudly.

Something lands with a crash.

"Damn!" The McGuire says.

Ranger and I reach the turkey barn. Ranger crouches behind it and I creep up beside him. We can see The McGuire's feet going back and forth behind his truck. It's lights shine on the side of the house.

"Stay down, that jacket is too bright," Ranger whispers.

Sandy barks from behind the house.

I bite my lip.

The McGuire turns the truck lights out and goes in the house.

"You go get Sandy," Ranger says. "I'm going to look in that freezer and see if the coins are still there."

"Ranger, be careful. It's close to the house."

"I'll hide if he comes out."

He slips away. I walk as quietly as I can round the house to Sandy who is sitting up, his ears pricked, tied to a post. I have my pocket knife out.

"It's okay, Sandy," I mutter. "I'm here to save you."

Sandy stands four-square to me and starts to bark.

I scramble back into the shadow behind the piled crates. I'm shaking: my jaw clenched so tight my teeth hurt.

A front window opens and The McGuire shouts, "Shut up, Sandy! Shut up!"

Sandy barks louder. McGuire shouts again, and Sandy finally quiets down. The window closes, and the curtains are drawn. The lights in the house go out.

I take a deep breath and dart out of the shadows, whispering, "Sandy, it's me, be quiet, you know me."

Sandy barks . . . and barks.

I dive back into the shadows, trip on a board, and fall on my face.

My stomach twists into a tight knot. I want to cry.

I crouch down in a huddle with my feet tucked under me. Then I wriggle round so I can see whatever awful thing is going to happen next.

The back door opens and The McGuire comes out.

"Shut up, you stupid dog," he yells. He peers around, and then comes into the yard. He has a bowl in one hand.

I bury my head in my arms and hold my breath. If The McGuire sees me, he'll crunch my bones into gravel and kick the pieces into the creek. And where is Ranger? If he's caught near the boxes he'll be stamped into a puddle.

The McGuire says, "Okay, here's your water."

Footsteps retreat toward the house. A door bangs shut. Silence.

I take a deep breath, run and crouch beside Sandy who is gulping water. I pat and stroke him, rub behind his ears. He goes on drinking. I whisper, "Good dog, Sandy. Good dog."

I cut his rope quickly.

My nose runs and I want to wipe it on my sleeve. Sandy sniffs my hand. I grab the rope-end and lead Sandy down the drive, pulling him gently.

Ranger comes back. "Those crates and boxes stink of turkey. He must be using them to move his birds," he whispers. "I checked the freezer and the coins are still there. Maybe we should take them too."

"We'll go back later."

A car comes down the hill; its lights sweep across The McGuire's yard. Ranger takes the rope and tries to move. Sandy pulls back.

"He won't come," Ranger says.

A light goes on in The McGuire's house.

I pick up Sandy. "We'll put him in the calf barn overnight," I whisper.

Sandy tries to lick my face. His breath stinks and I turn my head away. He licks my neck instead. A truck races towards us down the hill. Ranger dives into the bushes on one side of the road, I slide into the ditch on the other, with Sandy clasped against me, and his tongue tacky on my ear.

I lie still, listening for pounding feet, for The McGuire to come up the road yelling. I hear nothing.

Ranger slides down and lifts Sandy off me. He carries Sandy through the barnyard to the calf barn and into one of the pens. We've no pigs or calves in the barn right now. I put the light on and pull stale hay for Sandy's bedding from a broken bale and sit down to catch my breath.

Sandy lies down. He's scruffy and dirty. His ribs stick out, and there's a raw patch on his back. There is no hair round his neck. The rope must be too tight. I cut it off.

"I'll get dog food from the house," I say. "And you get some water."

"Okay, I'll fill a bucket and find a bowl."

I run to the garage. Moonlight makes the fence-posts silver and lays the shadows of the apple trees dark on the grass. I sneak into the basement and fill a couple of cans with dog food. Maybe I should stay with Sandy for the night? It would be best for him, scary for me.

When I get back to the barn, I put a quarter dish of dog food close to Sandy, who starts to gobble it up. Ranger has put down a beaten up enamel bowl of water.

"I've read that starving animals, or people, shouldn't stuff themselves with food too quickly," I tell Sandy. Then I sit down, my back to the door, watching him.

A voice behind me says, "So this is Sandy, The McGuire's dog."

CHAPTER 10

I GULP, TURN ROUND: MICHAEL IS leaning over the half-door.

I say, "It's Sandy, and he starves him, throws things at him, and it's not right ..."

Michael watches Sandy for a minute then comes in, bends down and, talking to him all the time, feels him all over. Sandy looks at him sideways, winces but goes on eating.

Michael is wearing a T-shirt, jeans and boots.

"Did I wake you up?" I ask just to break the silence. I pull my hair out of the collar of my jacket, twist it and chew the end.

"No, Tucker had to go out and I saw the light."

I hold my breath. What will Michael say?

Ranger rubs his nose. He has joined the two ends of the rope I'd cut from Sandy's neck in a knot.

Michael stands up, stares down at Sandy, and puts his hands in his pockets. "It *is* stealing, you know, even if it *is* Sandy."

"But, Michael . . ." I protest.

"Oh, I agree The McGuire shouldn't own a dog, or any other animal. Still, you've stolen his dog."

"He's Sandy . . ." I sniff. "He's Uncle Tam's dog. Can't we keep him?" I stroke Sandy.

"I don't see how we can." Michael sounds uncertain.

"Why not?" Ranger asks.

"Because Tucker and Sandy fight all the time," Michael says.

I'd like to ask Michael what to do about the gold coins in The McGuire's old freezer. Michael bends to stroke Sandy, and then says, "We'll have to tell Pa and Ma."

That decides me not to ask him about the coins: he'll tell Pa.

"He'll say we have to give him back," I protest.

"Um," says Michael, staring down at Sandy.

"Why can't we leave him in here for the night?" Ranger asks.

There's a scratching sound at the door: Tucker whines to come in.

"It's okay, Tucker," Michael calls as he sits down, wraps his arms round his knees, considering Sandy and us.

I twist my hair tighter. "Please, Michael, we *can't* give him back, Sandy needs food and care—and time."

"I'm not arguing with you," Michael says, "I'm thinking."

Sandy shuffles round in the hay, curls into a ball and closes his eyes. I reach out and stroke his head gently. He peers up at me, then closes his eyes again. I pull the hay closer around him and move the food and water so that he won't knock them over.

"We could put him in the hayloft for the night," Ranger says.

"No," says Michael, standing up, "we'll leave him here. No one will come in here tomorrow, or today, as it's Monday already. When I get to school, I'll ask Ellie if she can take him for a few days."

I jump up and hug Michael. "You're a genius."

"Good idea." Ranger stands up, stuffing the rope in his pocket.

Michael pushes me away. "It's after one o'clock in the morning and you better get to bed."

"You won't tell?" I ask.

"No." Michael sounds exasperated. "Just get to bed. I'm tired."

Ranger opens the door and Tucker slips in through the gap. Ranger grabs his collar and says, "Come on, Tucker, no visiting tonight."

Tucker snarls at Sandy who bares his teeth.

"That's what Tucker *always* says to Sandy," I say

contentedly. It confirms that Sandy really is Sandy.

Michael shrugs. "Pity we can't keep him." He leaves with Tucker. I stay where I am. Ranger goes out then comes back. "Come on, let's go to bed."

"I'm staying here to feed Sandy, and make sure he's okay," I say.

"Do you have to?"

"I think so, he needs to be looked after."

He frowns, rubs his nose. "Well, I'm going to bed."

"Tell Michael I'm here, okay?"

I watch him go to the house, but keep wanting to call him back.

The wind has risen and clouds begin to cover the stars and blur the moon; trees toss and bend. Thunderheads pile up in the west.

I close the half-doors and I lie down beside Sandy. His chocolate brown eyes are close to mine, his nose warm against my hand. His coat feels dull, almost greasy, though his skin is dry and flaky. He smells sour and his breath stinks.

The bare light bulb shines in my eyes, so I huddle down, tuck Sandy against me for warmth, and pull hay over us both. The walls creak as if someone were there. Maybe The McGuire followed us and knows I've got Sandy? He'd come in yelling, and he'd beat me and Sandy into mushy pulp.

94

Instead I hear the cows lumber past, brushing against the barn like giant hands trying to pick it up and toss it into the storm. There's a thundering noise on the metal roof: it's raining. I clutch Sandy tight as a gust of wind blows something across the yard with a rattle and it bangs against the calf-barn.

The rain wakes me a couple of times in the night between dreams of galloping across fields on Midnight. I give Sandy a handful of food each time, and go back to sleep curled round him.

A thumping and banging on the door wake me up again.

"It's me, Frame." Michael's voice is clear and urgent. "Get up and get to bed."

I struggle out of the hay and open the door. Michael stands there in rain and darkness, milking bucket in one hand, the cows behind him.

"Get to bed and I'll look after Sandy," he says, "I'll leave him with a chick-feeder so that he can eat during the day."

I creep upstairs to bed, pull the blankets over my head and fall into a deep well of warm quiet.

It seems I've been asleep for barely a minute when Ma calls me out of sleep and I get up, yawn hugely and see Dinah curled up with Squib on her bed. I change

95

and go downstairs to be greeted by the smell of coffee.

Ma breaks eggs into the big frying pan.

Michael bangs the front door as he comes in with the milk. I catch him by the coat cupboard and ask, "How's Sandy?"

"Fine."

Pa thumps into the house, his boots weighted with mud.

"Reuben," Ma shouts, "clean your boots."

He leaves the front door open while he scrapes the dirt off, then kicks his boots into the cupboard and comes into the kitchen.

"Hi, Frame." He ruffles my hair, almost pushing my nose onto my plate.

Ranger jumps down the stairs. Bird follows one step at a time, with Squib holding her hand. Squib perches on a stool beside me and sits Bear on the counter in front of her.

I look around and realize that, for them, nothing has happened and this is a normal Monday. It's me and Ranger who've had an adventure, but we can't share it.

Ma hands plates of eggs on toast to Squib, Bird and me. Squib holds her spoon high to let the yolk drip onto her plate.

Michael joins us, Tucker at his heel. Ranger gives

me a long look over his glass of juice. I grin.

Keeping a secret from my family will not be easy.

Bird takes a mouthful of egg. "Leo wants to come up here to meet you all."

"Are you serious about each other?" Pa asks.

"Yes."

Pa slathers marmalade on his toast. "When does Leo want to visit?"

"Soon. He wants to go night-fishing."

"Night-fishing?" Ma almost chokes on her coffee. "Whatever for?"

"He's Jamaican, they do it in Jamaica, and he wants to try it here."

"Where would he do it?" Ranger asks.

"Down along the river, I suppose," says Bird.

"He might catch a tree root or something . . ." I say with a shudder, thinking of Uncle Tam.

"I don't see a problem. Any weekend soon." Ma checks her watch and adds, "We'd better be going soon, Bird, if you're to catch that bus."

I don't want her to go. Even though she's not the way she was, she's still Bird, my sister.

She ruffles my hair as she stands up, the way Ma does. It's new coming from her, but I feel comforted. I put my spoon down to share a hug with her.

"I'll be back soon, with Leo," she says. Those

last two words take the edge off my sadness at her leaving. I'd like it better if Leo weren't coming back with her.

"I won't be gone long," she says. "And now I've got to finish packing up." She goes downstairs.

I sit down and eat quickly, then have to slow down: if I go to check on Sandy now everyone will see me. I cram in another piece of toast while everyone finishes.

Pa and Michael get ready to leave for school.

"Michael," I say, "don't forget..."

"Don't worry, I won't."

"Forget what?" Pa ties his shoelaces.

I don't hear Michael's answer as they leave.

Ma takes Squib upstairs to change her egg-splattered shirt. I collect my backpack, and put it in the front hall while I find my shoes and jacket. Last night's storm has left an overcast sky and a misty drizzle.

"I left a book in the barn," I call as I close the front door, giving Ma no time to ask "what book?"

I race across to the barn, jumping over cow pies in the yard. I fumble at the latch to the calf barn.

Sandy lies flat out in the hay. He lifts his head and I collapse on my knees beside him. Michael has filled both the water bowl and bucket and left an old chick-feeder full of dog food. Michael's the best.

"Good dog. Just stay quiet and don't bark." He licks my face. "I know . . . you're full of food . . . and you're happy to be with us, people you know."

I slip out of the barn and fasten the latch. Ranger meets me at the barn door with my backpack.

"He's fine," I say before he can ask.

"We can get a ride with Ma," Ranger says. "She's taking Bird to the bus stop."

Squib, Bird and Ma come out of the house, Squib carrying her blanket and Bear. Bird puts Squib into the centre seatbelt in the back and Ranger and I climb in beside her. Bird gets in the front.

As Ma drives down the road, she looks at us in the rear-view mirror, then asks, "How come so quiet this morning?"

Ranger says, "Nothing to say."

I say, "Thinking about The McGuire's dog."

Ranger nudges me and I blush: what a give-away.

Ma laughs and says, "I bet you dream about that dog."

"I did last night."

That gets me a poke from Ranger.

Bird turns to me and says, "You look like someone who's been up all night."

"The storm kept me awake."

"It was a bad one."

Ma drops us off at the school. We yell, "Goodbye!" And Bird and Squib wave as they drive off.

"I hope Michael finds a place for Sandy," I say.

Ranger says, "I hope so too."

CHAPTER 11

IN THE FIRST CLASS, SOCIAL STUDIES, I realize how tired I am. I have to prop my eyes open to stay awake. The morning goes by in a blur, trying not to sleep through classes. I find a quiet, if damp, corner of the playing field during recess and lunchtime and doze.

"Hey, you look like you crawled through a blizzard last night and forgot the way home." Amanda's voice wakes me with a start. She's wearing her brilliant red skirt and fluorescent yellow sweatshirt.

"I wish you'd wear sleepy colours," I say.

"Today is all gloom and doom and I want to bring some sunshine into the world," says Amanda.

"You do," I mutter.

"I don't think you've heard anything anyone said all day."

"The storm kept me awake."

"Whatever. You're up to something and I want to know what it is, because if you've been having adventures they've been ones that had you busy all night and that means fun," says Amanda. "And I've news, or no news, for you."

I open my eyes again but her clothes are too blinding so I shut them quickly.

"What's happened?"

"I talked to everyone I could think of, even the mail man and the vet and the guy who delivers the paper. No one has heard a thing about Sandy, they're just sorry no one knows where he is."

I open one eye. "If no one knows anything then no one has found him."

"Okay, it was fun detecting, but I agree that he must have drowned." She pulls my hair. "So, what have you been doing?"

I can't tell Amanda about the rescue. It'd be all over the school in five seconds. She may be my best friend, but she can talk the legs off twelve donkeys.

"Nothing's going on. What makes you think something's going on?"

There's a pause, then Amanda says, "Never mind, I guess you've got some weird secret . . . I'll find out in the end, I always do. But today I've got to go to the dentist after school. I hate the dentist, all poke and spit and poke."

"Is your dad picking you up?"

"Yes."

"Can Ranger and I ride with you to the end of Riverside Road? Then I won't have to walk all the way home."

"Okay," says Amanda. "And you better get some sleep before recess is over. If you go to sleep during class you might dream about lions and tigers and you might snore . . ."

Her voice fades into the distance. Recess ends, teachers give us homework, kids talk, and I forget what is said.

School finishes at last and I'm glad I'd asked Amanda for a ride because it's raining again. Her dad drops us off at the corner of Riverside.

Michael is standing there, where the high school bus stops. Rain drips off his nose and plasters his hair to his head. His jacket hangs soddenly and his jeans cling, soaked.

"Good thing you got a ride; if you'd walked I might have given up. What a pestiferous pair of nitwits you are." He sounds fed up. "Next time you two steal a dog, I'll have nothing to do with it—don't as much as hint that you've taken one." He hefts his pack onto his back and turns up Riverside.

"I'm glad you waited," I say, trying to make him feel better.

Michael strides ahead. "Fifteen minutes in this rain," he grumbles.

"I'm sorry."

He stops. "Just don't steal another dog."

"Never again," says Ranger.

I can't promise that: I might find another one starving and I couldn't walk away and do nothing.

Michael gives me a long frown and sighs. "You're hopeless, Frame."

"I didn't say anything," I say.

"Exactly." Michael marches off.

Ranger jogs after Michael and I run to catch up. My legs ache and all I want to do is to sit down.

"What about Sandy?" I ask Michael when we catch up.

"I'm going to take him over to Ellie's. She's got friends who want a dog, and she'll take Sandy to them."

"How do we get Sandy to Ellie?" Ranger asks.

"That's why I waited for you," says Michael. "You two cut down through the field behind the barns so you can't be seen from the house."

"What if Ma and Pa see us?" I worry.

"Just run fast."

He explains his plan. I try to give him a hug, but he shoves me away telling me not to get him any wetter.

Ranger and I cut down from the road to the calf barn. Rain gushes from the gutter at one end of the big barn. I splash through the mud of the barnyard, struggle to get the calf barn door open, and dive into the dimness of the pen. Ranger almost steps on my heels; he closes the barn door.

"Don't turn the light on," I say.

Sandy stands in the hay, and then backs up against the wall.

"It's okay, Sandy, it's okay." I wait until my eyes adjust to the half-light, then move toward him. I drop to my knees beside him, stroke and talk to him gently.

"Be quiet, Sandy. Don't bark," I whisper, scratching behind his ears.

I wrap Sandy in my jacket and we leave the barn. The wind catches the door and slams it shut behind us. We go as fast we can back past the barns, up the field to the top gate.

Michael pulls in beside us. Sandy licks my face. Ranger opens the car door and I put Sandy on the front seat.

"Leave it . . . leave your jacket," says Michael. "You're soaked anyway."

Michael leans over and pushes me out of the car. "McGuire's truck . . . coming up the hill, I can see him in the mirror." He pulls away, gravel spurting out behind the wheels.

A truck pulls up beside us. The McGuire leans across the front seat, winds the window down, and says, "Have you seen my dog?"

I stand behind Ranger, face down, avoiding The McGuire's eyes.

"You, girl, have you seen my dog?"

I shake my head.

The McGuire sniffs and glances down the road. "Thought I saw a dog in that car."

"Michael's taking ours to the vet," Ranger says.

I'm shaking all over.

The McGuire grunts and narrows his eyes. He winds the window up and drives away. Piled boxes and an old bike frame wobble in the bed of his truck.

Ranger's and my eyes meet, and I smile shakily. Then we start to laugh and laugh.

"Come on, let's get home before The McGuire comes back," Ranger says. "You look a mess."

We trudge down the field. My shoes are full of water and I don't worry about stepping in puddles as we go through the barnyard to the house.

We leave our wet shoes and backpacks in the coat cupboard. Home feels warm and smells of fresh baked cookies. Ranger gets to the kitchen first and takes two cookies from the rack. I snatch one.

We hear our truck pulling into the driveway. Ma comes in with Squib. "Did you walk all the way home, Frame? You look like a drowned cat—go and change."

My stomach is still tied in knots and rebels at the third cookie, so I give it to Tucker.

Michael arrives home just before dinner with my jacket. I give him a hug and a wink to thank him for helping to rescue Sandy.

When we're at the dinner table, Ma leans forward, fork in hand, and says, "It looks like the police are still on the trail of who killed Uncle Tam."

"What's happened?" Ranger asks.

"I was talking to Seth's mum at quilting this morning. She said the police have been up and down the river, and up Riverside Road again," says Ma. "And they've been poking in barns and places like that."

"Did they poke around The McGuire's place?" I ask.

"I wonder if we live across the road from a murderer?" says Ranger. I kick him under the table. "He's a gut-griper, up to anything."

Squib sings, "Griper piper pudding and pie," and tips her peas on the floor.

The phone rings. I pick it up and it's Bird.

"Bird says she's coming next weekend with Leo. He still wants to go night-fishing."

"Great! Let's hope the weather's good," Ma says.

I wish things could be the way they used to be between Bird and me. That's a dim hope, with her bringing Leo home.

I sprawl on the chesterfield in the sitting room trying to finish *The Incredible Journey*, but fall asleep before I've read two words.

A knock at the front door wakes me up. I stretch, yawn, and peer over the back of the chesterfield. The knocking gets louder. I get up, go and open the door. Pa comes to the top of the basement stairs as I go past.

The McGuire stands there. I freeze.

"You, kid, have you taken my dog? He got cut loose last night."

I shake my head, speechless. He's big and broad. His anger burns towards me like a fire. Talking to people I don't know is bad; an angry person I can't deal with at all.

Pa stands beside me. "What kind of dog?" he asks.

"A terrier."

He calls out to Ma, "Bea, have you seen Mr. McGuire's dog? It's a terrier."

"No, I haven't," she calls back.

The McGuire leans on the door-jamb, pokes his head in and says, "Barks a lot, bites—got cut loose last night. I saw her poking around my place with her brother." He jerks his thumb at me. "He got cut loose last night."

Pa steps in front of me.

"We've not seen him," says Pa.

"Fine. If you do, let me know."

"We'll give you a call," says Pa.

"I'm asking around," says The McGuire. "Your kids asked about him when they cleaned my barn."

"We'll keep an eye out for him," says Pa.

"Umph," says The McGuire, and stalks off into the darkness.

CHAPTER 12

PA CLOSES THE DOOR. HE STANDS for a moment with his hand on the knob. Then he moves to the front window and looks out, shading his face against the reflections. He turns to look at me, puts a firm hand on my shoulder, and guides me back to the sitting room. He calls Ranger, who comes upstairs.

"Ranger and Frame," says Pa, standing with his hands deep in his jeans' pockets, feet apart. "Tell me about the dog."

Ranger and I look at each other.

"Do you know where the dog is?"

"No." I take a quick look at Ranger. We'll have to say that it's Sandy.

"You know something about it, so tell me."

So we tell Pa in bits and pieces, about Sandy being tied up, no hair on his neck, ribs sticking out.

"And his breath stinks," I say, adding, "Michael knows where he is."

"Michael!" Pa shouts. I wish I was invisible.

Michael comes in.

"Where's The McGuire's dog?" Pa asks.

"He's with a family north of Duncan, friends of Ellie's. I don't know them."

Pa sighs. "How'd you get mixed up in this?"

"He was starving. He was certainly one sick dog." Michael rubs a hand through his hair.

"It was my idea," I say. "We rescued him."

"I'm sure it was," says Pa. "He was being mistreated, and you couldn't leave him there, right?"

"Yes."

"And why? Why? Why didn't you just phone the S.P.C.A. and tell them about Sandy?" Pa asks.

I look at Ranger, Ranger looks at Michael. I shuffle my feet, Ranger rubs his nose.

Michael sticks his hands in his pockets. "I didn't think of it."

Pa chews his lower lip, jiggles the keys in his pocket. "Okay, you rescued Sandy. Nevertheless, the way you did it was wrong. You have to apologize to Mr. McGuire for taking the dog, even if Sandy used to be Tam's dog."

"Then he should apologize to the Dakens," I protest.

"What do you mean?"

"Er . . . at his place . . . he's got . . ." And I stop.

Ranger rubs his nose and makes a face at me. "He's got the Dakens' gold coins at his place. We found them when we were shovelling crap."

"And you chose not to tell us, or the police, about them?"

I scuff the floor with one foot and say. "Well, we *were* snooping."

"And you got into trouble once for doing that," He sighs. "Trying to get a straight story out of you two is like wringing water out of a stone. Anyway, you're grounded: no helping at the Dakens' or horse-riding or Scouts for a month." He studies Ranger and me. "And you will apologize to Mr. McGuire before the end of this week."

"Yuck," I say. Ranger groans.

"I'll tell the police where the coins are," Pa says. "They can take it from there."

To make it worse, after dinner Michael pulls me into the sitting room and says quietly, "Ellie's friends are having trouble getting Sandy to eat."

"Oh no." I gulp. "Can they feed him with a dropper?"

"More likely a spoon, or bread dipped in water. They like him though."

I go to bed and worry about Sandy.

And right after school the next day, Pa says, "I've told the police and they will follow up about the coins." He pulls his jacket from the rack. "But Frame, Ranger, we're going down to The McGuire's right now. Come on."

I swallow hard. But Pa means it. So Ranger and I keep our jackets on and go down the road with Pa. The grey skies look just how I feel.

The McGuire's truck is in. My breath comes fast. I push my hands deep into my pockets.

The McGuire, loading turkey crates into his truck, sees us coming up his driveway.

He looks surprised to see us and says. "So what're you here for?"

"They've got something to say to you." Pa pushes us forward.

"I'm sorry we took your dog," says Ranger.

The McGuire wears scruffy runners like mine. I make fists deep in my pockets, twist my feet in the dirt and say, "And I'm sorry I thought . . . I mean, I'm sorry too."

"Why did you take him then, eh?" he asks.

I sneak a quick look at him under my eyebrows. His plaid shirt falls away from a stained T-shirt.

"Why?" he repeats.

"Because he was sick . . . because he was Uncle

Tam's . . . because I wanted him to be well again and . . ." I run out of breath.

"Why didn't you come and ask about him instead of snooping?" The McGuire leans against the truck and hooks his thumbs into his belt loops. I tuck myself in close behind Ranger's shoulder.

"He's a good dog, Sandy. Seth asked me to look after him when he took over Tam's place, said he kept biting him. But I couldn't get him to eat. I believe he was pining for Tam."

"Pining? Oh, but..." I say, horrified. Was everything I thought a mistake? "So he wasn't starved?"

"Damn it, kid, you thought I was starving him?"

"But," I say, "he ate and ate and ate when we had him overnight."

"You're family, he knows you."

I grab Ranger's wrist. "Michael said he's not eating at his new home."

"Sounds like you better have him at your place," says The McGuire.

"He and Tucker, they fight." I say to The McGuire's T-shirt.

"Get them used to each other," says The McGuire. "Takes time, but it can be done." He hitches his pants up. "You kids did a good job of mucking out that barn for me. Okay if I call you next time I need it done?"

"Sure," says Ranger. My heart hits my boots: that stink all over again?

"And don't you imagine I starve animals—I don't." He pauses, scratches his stomach. "Eh, girl?"

I shuffle my feet in the dirt. I clench my fists tight, look him right in the face, and say, "I'm really, really sorry. I just didn't understand."

It rains off and on for the next two days. On Thursday I get eighty percent on the social studies quiz about tigers, which makes me happy. Amanda stays for band practice after school, so Ranger and I start walking home. I chew my ponytail.

"What do you think the police will do when they . . .?" I begin to ask Ranger. Right then, Seth pulls up beside us. He winds down the window and says, "Hop in, I'll drive you home."

"No, Ranger," I whisper in his ear. "We need to talk . . . just us."

"It's not raining right now," Ranger says to Seth, "so we'll walk home."

"How's everything?" Seth asks. "Did you manage with math yesterday?"

"I squeaked a pass," I say.

"Well done."

He asks when Bird is coming home.

"Tomorrow," I say.

"Maybe I'll stop by sometime," he says.

"Er . . . her boyfriend's coming with her."

"Makes no difference, she's still *my* girl." He winds the window up and drives on.

"I bet he's going to The McGuire's," says Ranger.

"Could be," I say. "But anyway, what do you think the police will do when they find the coins?"

"Stick The McGuire in jail for a few years," he says,.

"It'll be a thousand years when they discover that he killed Uncle Tam."

"*If* he killed Uncle Tam."

"Well, he's got the coins, so he must have," I say.

Ranger kicks gravel at the side of the road. "Someone might have hidden them there."

"Why?"

"Because it's a great place to hide stuff. It's a mess; you could hide the Crown Jewels in there."

"But we found the coins," I say.

"We were snooping."

I'm still convinced that The McGuire is the villain, that no one else could have killed Uncle Tam.

We get to our driveway and run to the front door.

Over juice and cookies, Ma says she heard that The McGuire had been taken in for questioning by the police.

"Well, Pa told them about the coins," says Ranger.

The McGuire will know that it was us that found the coins in his old freezer!

"He'll pound us into mush." I shiver.

"I wonder if the coins were still there," says Ranger. "Let's hope The McGuire doesn't come after us with a pitchfork."

"He might have moved them," I say.

Pa and Ma are out for the evening. Michael has his stamp catalogues out. Ranger carries on as if nothing has happened, grumbles because he can't go to Scouts, and does homework. I get my books out on the coffee table in the sitting room and work on math. The numbers tumble into jumbled piles in my head.

Finch Dakins calls and I tell him I can't come and help with the horses because I'm grounded. I finish my homework and grouch my way to bed. I can see another week going by and me not being allowed to ride.

I wake up to clear blue skies, which matches my mood: Bird is coming home this evening. School goes quickly and I get a ride home with Amanda and her dad.

I eat a couple of cookies, staring out of the window at the calf-barn. Will Sandy start eating and be alright at his new home? Or should we bring him here, get Tucker and Sandy used to each other? I sigh, collect my books, and try to study at the dining room table.

I'm half listening for the sound of a car in the driveway. Will Bird have time to talk to me properly? Or will Leo get in the way? Will he keep her to himself? I chew my pencil: what does he look like? I drift into memories of Bird and I talking, sharing clothes.

"They're here!" Ma's shout interrupts my thoughts. I run to meet them at the door. Squib's there, and Bird appears with a huge dark presence behind her: Leo. His smile hangs in the shadows above Bird's head.

Bird gives my ponytail a tug and says, "This is my boyfriend, Leo."

Bird swings Squib up and hands her to Leo. He is bigger, taller and broader than Ma. Bird comes about half-way up Leo's chest.

At dinner, Leo asks, "Can we really go night-fishing?"

"Tomorrow night would be good," says Ma.

"I've got everything ready," Pa says.

"Will you go too, Bird?" Ma asks.

"No, I'll stay home with Squib. I've an essay to do."

"There'll be no moon tomorrow night," says Ma.

"A pitch black night is best, then the fish can't see you," says Leo. Bird smiles at him and he touches her hand.

"We can go too, can't we?" Ranger says.

"You're grounded," Pa says.

"Let them go," Ma says. "They've apologized and this is special."

"Thanks, Ma," I say.

Ma helps herself to more green beans.

"Michael, will you come too?" I ask.

"I'm going out with Ellie," Michael says.

So it'll be Ma, Ranger, me, and Leo.

Leo seems to know all about night fishing. He tells us how, back home, they shine a light on the water to attract the fish.

"Go down to the bridge by Piercy's place," Pa says. "That's where the fish are."

That gives me a jolt. That's above the bend where we found Uncle Tam.

I think Leo is holding Bird's hand under the table. Bird is drifting further and further away from me.

Ma takes Squib up to bed, rejoining us for dessert.

We play card-games until bed-time. I'm so tired I don't remember going to sleep.

119

It's a good thing it's Saturday, because when I wake up it's already ten o'clock.

There's a smell of garlic in the kitchen: Bird brought garlic sausages for us. There's one left in the fridge and I fry it with leftover porridge. Everyone else has eaten and the house is quiet, apart from Leo and Bird talking in the basement.

The front door bangs open and Ranger shouts, "Let's play baseball. It stopped raining."

I help him find bats, bases, and boots. Even Leo joins us and we play a riotous game in the wet grass and thin sunshine. We take turns to bat or pitch. No one wins, and Michael ends by sliding through a cow pie and stomping back to the house in a huff.

The rest of us, loaded with equipment, gather by the barn, and Leo asks where my name comes from. Ma laughs.

I look at Leo's feet and say, "Ma was hanging pictures a week before I was due and dropped a frame on the bulge that was me. I was born that night."

"That's a good reason for a name with a difference," says Leo.

Not too many people ask, but it's always people I don't know and it's difficult to tell them.

CHAPTER 13

MICHAEL, WEARING CLEAN JEANS, meets us at the front door with car keys in his hand.

"I'll be working at the auction," he says. "Then Ellie and I are going to a party."

I watch Michael get in the truck. I want him to know I'm grateful for his help with Sandy. I run down and bang on the truck window. He rolls it down.

"Have a great time." I give him a lop-sided smile.

He laughs.

"Frame yourself," he says, the way he used to when I was Squib's age.

I wave him out the driveway and go back into the house. Everyone is around the dining table, talking, laughing, eating. I join them.

After lunch, Bird and Leo go for a walk. Ma works in the garden. Ranger listens to Bruce Springsteen downstairs while practising knots for Scouts.

I sit on the bottom of the stairs to watch, then ask, "Do you think The McGuire will try to take revenge on us because we told about the coins?"

"The police would have found out somehow in the end." Ranger twists the string into a half-hitch round one finger. "So I can't see him doing anything."

I scratch my head. "Why do you think The McGuire didn't tell anyone about having Sandy?"

"Well, he told us." Ranger ties another knot.

"If it's not a secret, how come no one heard about him having Sandy?" It's as bad as math: the questions tumble into different answers every time, and none of them make any sense.

"I don't know . . . but he's guilty of *some*thing." Ranger undoes the knot he'd made.

"He's guilty that Uncle Tam died, that's for sure," I say. "I wish he looked guilty though."

"People don't go round looking guilty, not even us when we snooped at The McGuire's place." Ranger ties another knot.

"I suppose that's true."

Pa and Squib come home then. A stretch of fencing at the far side of the top field needs fixing and Pa needs help so Squib and I go with him. Squib passes tools and watches birds. Huge clouds chase across the sky all afternoon and a chill wind blows.

When we come in I lie on the floor and read. Dinah sits in the middle of my back.

Pa makes three huge pizzas for dinner. We eat them all, even with Michael gone. Conversation flows round me while I stay quiet. I watch Leo sitting opposite, beside Bird. I notice how he fits in with Bird, how he's easy with the family, and the family with him. I feel separate from them.

Ma asks Leo how many there are in his family. He has four sisters, three brothers, and grandparents living at home.

"We cut sugar cane or pick fruit in season," says Leo.

"Do you pick pineapples?" Ranger asks.

Bird and Leo laugh and Leo says, "Yes."

After dinner we search out fishing rods, flashlights, boots, and flasks of hot chocolate, and put them in the trunk of the car. Ranger and I pile into the back seat and wind the windows down.

At the top of the driveway I realize I should have put Bird's jacket on over my extra sweater; I ask Ma to stop so I can get it. I run indoors, yell to Bird that I'm borrowing her jacket, seize it from the cupboard, shoving my arms in the sleeves on my way out.

A truck coming down the road catches me in the sweep of its headlights as I get back in the car. Ma pulls out onto the road. The rush of cold air tugs at my hair; it's rich with the smell of wet earth and mysterious creatures. Riding Midnight would give me the same excitement. Is imagining better than the real thing? That's a strange thought and I put it away: I want a horse.

Ma parks close to the bridge and we get out, sort through the rods, deciding who should have which.

Ranger leads the way down the bank. Leo tries to help me but I don't need help. I have my flashlight and grab a thin trunk or branch as I scramble down.

We find places along the river, close to the bridge, the opposite side from the Piercy's. I perch on a rock close to the trail, glad I'm wearing three pairs of socks.

It's spooky: someone could reach out from the shadows and I wouldn't know until their hands grabbed me. I blot out those thoughts and focus on fishing.

Time blurs, runs away like the river. Pictures of Sandy, of Uncle Tam lassoing a calf and of The McGuire lifting boxes float through my mind. My line tugs and slacks with the flow of water.

Ma, to my left, calls, "How're you doing, kids?"

I wriggle my shoulders. "My feet are cold."

A truck stops by the bridge; the truck door opens and slams shut.

"I'm okay," Ranger shouts.

"Leo?"

"Just wondering why I thought this was a good idea." He's between me and Ma.

Ma chuckles. "Because you wanted to feel Canadian cold?"

There's movement on the trail behind me: someone is slithering and sliding down. Is it The McGuire? The hair at the back of my neck begins to prickle. I edge along my rock towards the bridge.

I cower back into the bush behind me and put my head in my arms. It must be The McGuire, come for revenge. A thin blade of light crosses my legs, steadies, moves upward, and is put out. I can't see.

I'm terrified rigid, like a rabbit caught in headlights. My fishing rod rattles against the bush. I let go of it, scared into my bones. My throat closes, tight.

I'm picked up and crushed against the heavy woollen smell of a man's coat. Someone's breath touches my face. I smell peppermint.

"My girl, you are, my very own girl." It's *Seth* breathing words into my hair.

I kick him, hard, push back and yell, "It's me, Frame. *I'm not Bird.*"

His grip changes to my shoulders and he shakes me. I try to kick him, to pummel him with my fists.

"You . . . you . . . stupid, meddling little sneak!" he hisses.

He shakes me so hard I'm sure my teeth rattle. My hands swing out.

"You . . . weasel," Seth growls.

I shriek, "Ma! Ranger!"

"You found the coins, didn't you? Ruined everything for me, you did, on purpose," Seth hisses. "Sneak . . . snoop. Now you're pretending to be Bird, just to get me all messed up."

He thought I was Bird because I'm wearing her jacket!

Ma shouts, "I'm coming!" Her flashlight cuts the thin scrub.

"I'll chuck you in the river right now," Seth continues. "So you'll end up like Tam."

I claw and scratch Seth's hands, face. I can't get away, can't escape. He's hauling me round, down, towards the river.

There's a rustling, someone coming fast, from upriver. Then someone—Ranger—tears at Seth.

"Leave her alone!" Ranger pounds Seth.

Seth laughs, deep in his throat. He shakes me again, hard.

I reach for Ranger one-handed, and snatch at his jacket. Then there's a huge dark shadow on my other side. Leo grabs Seth, shoves an elbow into me, sends me back into the undergrowth, hurtles Seth sideways, toward the river.

His arms and legs windmill, whip bushes. He goes into the rush of water.

I'm shaking all over. Seth thrashes downstream. There's another splash, then nothing except the wind and the run of the river.

CHAPTER 14

MA BURSTS OUT OF THE BUSHES, panting. She reaches across Leo and pulls me to her. "You okay, Frame?"

"Sorry I took so long, Mrs. Williams," says Leo, "I got tangled in my line. I'll go check on that guy." Leo turns downstream and vanishes into darkness.

"It . . . it was Seth," I whisper.

"Seth!" Ranger and Ma exclaim together.

I snuffle and cry into Ma's shoulder, wrap my arms and legs round her, and hang on tight. She sits down and holds me.

"He thought I was Bird . . . because I'm wearing her jacket." I gulp. Gradually I stop crying and shaking. The horrors melt into Ma's warmth. I sniff and wipe my face on her sleeve.

"We'd better call the police." Ma loosens her grip and I slide off her knee. "And we'd better tell the Piercys; they've probably heard the racket and are wondering what on earth's going on."

I shudder.

"I can go tell the Piercys, Ma," says Ranger.

"We'll go together." Ma stands up. "I'll call the police from there."

There's shouting and splashing downstream. I grab Ma's hand and we listen for a minute. I quiver. Seth might come back. Then Ranger turns and starts up the trail. His flashlight silhouettes his legs and fishing rod.

I climb the bank without thinking, still in that black place with Seth's laugh. I gulp and sniff, wipe my nose with one hand.

Ma erupts with anger behind me. She mutters, "... idiot ... beat the daylights ... wicked ... scaring a child ... Seth ..." Halfway up she asks, "Frame, what happened to your rod?"

The question jolts me out of the unreality of the past minutes, and I think back.

"I dropped it. I think Leo picked it up . . . I don't know where he put it. And I've lost my flashlight."

"We'll come back and get everything tomorrow ... kick Seth into next week . . . that lunkhead . . ." Ma fumes behind me.

She takes my hand as we reach the top of the bank and cross the road. Seth's truck is so close to our car that Ma has trouble getting in.

I try not to think about Seth. Something itches in the back of my mind about the smell of peppermint. I wish I could catch the memory.

Then a boiling black rage snakes through me. I want to hit something, anything. My heart thuds so hard it might burst out of my chest. My stomach knots tight as a drum: anger at Seth for trying to drown me.

Ma drives down Piercy's driveway and parks. Stephie leans out of an upstairs window, yelling and waving. I turn and give a small wave so she knows I've seen her. Mrs. Piercy stands in the driveway beside the house. She glances at us and then turns back towards the river where a whale fight seems to be happening.

"I've called the police." Mrs. Piercy twists her hands together. "I called when I first heard shouting and then splashing."

Ma asks, "How long before they get here?"

"We were out with the sheep, so they shouldn't be long. We thought it was poachers."

Ma explains about the night-fishing and Seth's attack. Mrs. Piercy is horrified.

We go to the fence and stare down towards the river. The fight seems to be slowing down, but not the shouting. I'm barely conscious of Ma and Mrs. Piercy talking behind us: fury at Seth burns me.

Down near the river, there's more splashing and cursing, then Leo shouts, "Got him!"

"That girl," a half-choked voice says. There's the sound of vomiting.

I want to go home. Mr. Piercy pushes through the gate from the pasture. His shoes squelch and he's wet from the waist down. Leo, wet from top to toe, follows with an arm-lock on Seth Curzon, whose jacket hangs in wet tatters. Blood runs in trickly streaks down one side of his face. I don't care. In fact, I'm glad. He scared me right to my toes.

They pause on the edge of the light.

Seth sees me. He lunges forward, twisting in Leo's grip. "That girl, I thought she was Bird, my girl."

"She's not your girl," says Leo.

"I *told* you," I say.

"You messed up everything," Seth says. "You poked around, asking foolish questions, looking for Sandy." Seth wrenches at Leo again. "I should have drowned that dog with Tam."

No one moves or speaks. I can hear the river, the wind loud in the trees. A shoe grates on gravel. I see only Seth Curzon. I know him. I've ridden with him, talked with him in the farmyard. I'm cold, frozen inside.

Behind us, a police car comes down the driveway, catching us in its lights. The car stops and two officers

131

get out, the ones who came to the house before: Crooked Lace and Muddy Shoe.

"He knows about how Uncle Tam died, he just said so." Ranger shouts at the policemen and points at Seth.

"I didn't . . ." Seth starts with a shout but his voice tapers into silence.

The officers look at Ranger then at all of us. Then Crooked Lace says, "We were called about poachers, so what's going on?"

I say, "Uncle Tam saw him . . ."

Ranger shouts, "He killed Uncle Tam . . ."

Ma says, "He tried to drown . . ."

Mr. Piercy says, "He fell in . . ."

Stephie shouts from the window, "They had a fight . . ."

Leo says, "He tried to push . . ."

Everyone talks, shouts, tries to explain, all at once, while Seth stands and drips. Muddy Shoe holds his hands up and slowly, very slowly, quiet comes.

He says. "Who made the call?"

"I did," says Mrs. Piercy.

Mr. Piercy explains about the splashing in the river, concern for their sheep, going to see what was going on, finding Leo and Seth, and hauling Seth up to the house.

Ma tells how Seth scared me, and how he said he should have drowned that dog with Uncle Tam.

Crooked Lace moves toward Seth, and takes hold of one arm; Leo has the other twisted up behind Seth's back.

Crooked Lace says, "I think you'd better come with us. I'm detaining you to answer questions about disturbing the peace, for one thing. There maybe other areas of interest as well; we'll see."

"Do you need a witness?" Leo asks.

"We'd appreciate that," says Muddy Shoe.

I remember what it was about the smell of peppermint. I have to tell Crooked Lace, but how? And when?

Ma steps forward. "I'll take the kids home. Leo, come with us, change and then go into Duncan."

Mr. Piercy says, "Leo, I'll pick you up when I'm dry, and we'll go together."

"Thanks," says Ma.

"Come as soon as you can," says Crooked Lace.

I reach out and poke his arm.

"Yes?" He says.

I rub one foot up and down my leg, and dig my hands deep in my pockets. "Um . . . er . . . did you keep the things I gave you . . . at the hospital . . . when Ranger cut himself?"

Crooked Lace sounds puzzled. "I believe we did. Why?"

"I think there . . . um . . . were mint wrappers in there," I say, watching his feet. One lace is crooked again.

"Is that important?" He asks.

"Seth Curzon . . . he smells of peppermint," I say. "I could smell it when he tried to throw me in the river." My hands are clenched into fists and I'm blushing. Ma wraps one arm round me and gives me a hug.

"Well done, kid," Crooked Lace says. I sneak a peek at his face. He's smiling at me, a wide, pleased grin.

In a rush, I say, "Uncle Tam . . . the calf tangled in the halter rope . . . cutting the calf free . . ." I scuff my feet in the gravel.

Seth's shoulders slump.

I can't stop, I have to tell what happened. I stare at Muddy Shoes' feet so that I won't be distracted, so that I can tell the story. "He must have seen Seth coming from Dakens' place, down to the foot-bridge."

Ma gasps and I pause, catch my breath.

"Uncle Tam must have chased and caught him," says Ranger. "And they had a fight."

He stops, I give him a quick look of gratitude, then I finish the story. "And that's how Seth got hold of the knife," I rub one foot up and down my leg. "And killed Uncle Tam."

"And then he pushed Uncle Tam in the river," Ranger finishes.

"Mercy's sake!" says Mrs. Piercy.

"It wasn't supposed to happen," Seth says. "It was just a fight . . . but he fell."

"What day did this happen?" Muddy Shoe asks.

"February 10th . . . as if I'd forget," Seth says.

Muddy Shoe checks his note book. "The night of the break-in at Dakens'?"

Seth nods.

"You were on the Dakens' property?" Muddy Shoe asks.

Seth nods again.

"So what was the fight about?" Crooked Lace asks.

"He'd cut the calf free . . . he saw me with the bag of coins . . ." Seth twists against Leo's and Crooked Lace's grip on his arms. "He came at me . . . at the footbridge . . . yelling my name . . . he knew it was me."

Seth stares into the darkness. "He tried to stop me . . . to take the bag away . . . his knife open in his hand . . . we fought . . ."

"And you got hold of the knife?" Muddy Shoe asks.

"It wasn't like that." Seth shakes his head. "I had to stop him yelling . . . the knife twisted up . . . up into him . . . between us." He gulps. "Blood on his shirt, I saw it as he went backwards . . . into the river."

I bite the inside of my cheeks. I don't want to cry. Seth looks over his shoulder, towards the river.

"The current took him fast . . . I couldn't do anything . . . Too sore, too winded, too beat up." He sniffs, gulps, as if he's crying. "I threw the knife after him . . . couldn't . . . didn't want to keep it."

CHAPTER 15

I'M PICTURING UNCLE TAM IN THE river, his jacket moving in the current, the way I found him.

"So she's right, eh?" says Crooked Lace. "He caught you. You fought . . . and killed him?"

"No . . . I mean, yes we fought . . . but it was an accident," Seth shouts, butting his head forward, twisting away from Crooked Lace. He stops, sniffs. "It wasn't supposed to happen like that. He was a good guy."

I twist my shoulders, look at Ranger, then mutter, "We found the rope . . . the halter Uncle Tam cut loose."

"What do you mean?" Crooked Lace asks.

"Er . . . we found the end of the halter." I twist one foot in the dirt. "It's tangled . . . stuck, in the river." I gulp. "We couldn't get it free . . . we pulled and pulled . . ."

"Dear heaven, what next?" says Ma.

"Whereabouts in the river?" Muddy Shoe asks.

"Opposite Dakens' place," I say. "On Uncle Tam's side of the river, near the footbridge . . . that's how Uncle Tam must have seen Seth"

"The rope's caught under the bank," says Ranger.

"Anything else?" Crooked Lace asks.

"No." I stare at his feet. "Well yes, I hid the other half of the halter behind the bales . . . in the hayloft."

"And, Mr. Curzon, you hid the gold coins you stole at Mr. McGuire's place?" Muddy Shoe says.

"He didn't know," Seth says. "The place is such a mess I thought they'd be safe."

"What about Sandy?" I shout, angry all over again. He talks of the gold coins and The McGuire as if Sandy didn't matter. "You gave Sandy to The McGuire so he'd starve to death?"

Seth shrugs. "I asked Brice to keep him because, after Tam died, he kept trying to bite me. Then I wouldn't dare sell the coins, because it was in the paper that they'd been stolen."

"You came out the back of the Dakens' place, going to the footbridge?" Ma asks. "You were going across the river to Tam's place?" Ma asks.

"Er . . . yes," Seth says.

"You were going to steal from Tam as well?" Ma hisses. "You rotten, cheap, miserable lump of deceit."

"Fumet," I say softly.

"Boil-brained," says Ranger, not so softly.

Seth shrugs. "I wanted money to give Bird a present."

"Okay, that's enough." Muddy Shoe pushes Seth toward his car. "Mr. Curzon, you're coming with us."

Crooked Lace says, over his shoulder to Leo, "See you in half an hour or so, okay? We'll hear the details then. And we'll come out and get the rope on Monday."

Mrs. Piercy pushes her husband towards the house and shouts at Stephie to get back to bed.

Ma hustles Ranger and me to the car. "You two put the rods and flashlights into the trunk. Leo, you must be frozen. Get in the front."

"I'm dripping." Leo's teeth chatter and he shakes with cold.

"That's okay, get in and get close to the heat."

Ranger and I clear the back seat then scramble in. I'm quivery with excitement.

"Holy wow!" says Ranger.

Ma starts the car, turns it and heads for home.

"We discovered who killed Uncle Tam," I say and then stop: the villain is someone I know. I don't know how I feel about him: sad, let down, uncertain? I don't know even how to *think* about Seth. I fall onto Ranger when we go round a corner.

Ranger pushes me off and asks, "What will happen to Seth?"

"He'll get jail time," says Ma. "Probably for manslaughter, for stealing . . . other things too."

"Are we witnesses?" I hang onto the seat belt as Ma takes the next corner.

"I think so."

"We heard what he said, about the coins and everything, and that must be evidence," I say.

The moon comes out. Long banners of cloud chase across the sky, leaving patches of light over the valley where shadows leap at us like Halloween goblins and race away like a herd of wild horses. Is Midnight with the herd? Will I own a horse one day? He's a dream galloping into the night.

Ma drives the winding road home and I see the rush of trees, bushes, and a field. They are there everyday, but tonight the earth stands clean and huge and I want to reach out and grab it, taste it, smell it. So much has happened tonight yet the sky and the earth do what they've always done.

"Thank you for rescuing me, Leo." I'm shy saying that, though I'm deeply grateful.

He turns and smiles at me, his teeth gleaming in the shadows of the car. "It was almost a pleasure," he says.

We all laugh. I'm glad he's with us.

I can't make sense of my feelings about Seth. "Ma, I thought Seth Curzon was an okay kind of person, so how come he did horrid things?" I clench my fists.

"There aren't enough bad words to describe how I feel about him right now," Ma says.

"He likes horses," I say. "But he killed Uncle Tam . . . He's a villain."

"Piece of fumet," says Ranger.

I give a horrified gasp. "I had The McGuire all wrong!" I exclaim.

"Me too," says Ranger.

"It's me that's boil-brained," I say. "I thought The McGuire killed Uncle Tam, and he didn't. I thought he stole the Dakens' gold coins, and he didn't. And," I wail, "I thought he was starving Sandy, and he wasn't."

"Easy to get mistaken by people," says Leo. I can hear his teeth chattering with cold.

"I guess The McGuire's not as bad as I thought." I say.